Andrew (A to Z)

a novel

by

K. B. Dixon

Publisher: Baffling Bay Books

ISBN 978-1-7346759-1-7

1 3 5 7 9 10 8 6 4 2

Also by K.B. Dixon:

The Sum of His Syndromes

My Desk and I

For Sandra Jean

A

Arizona

There is a rumor I was born there, but I don't believe it. I don't feel like a person who was born in Arizona, I feel like a person who was born somewhere else—somewhere with trees and an ocean and a liberal political tradition. Somewhere like Washington or Oregon or Massachusetts.

Abelia

A semi-deciduous flowering shrub. We have five of them growing along the rock wall that separates our property from Daniel Boyd's. While I rarely see this neighbor to my west, I know he is there and that's enough to disturb my day. I don't like him. I can't say why exactly. My reaction is visceral. There is something about his loose-jointed demeanor; his slack, hounddoggy face; his infantilized self-absorption that I find deeply offensive. I know little about him—only that he is divorced and that he works for a computer company.

Accordion

I was surprised to see a man playing one the other

day. It seems like something from another age—the instrumental equivalent of a pterodactyl.

Acquisitive

We are obviously an acquisitive group here in this neighborhood and some of us are more acquisitive than others, but there is something about the nature of Boyd's particular species of getting that is especially off-putting. I think in part it is simply how much he has (his garage is a disgrace), but it is also what he has. It is not age-appropriate. Flabby, balding, and fifty-five if he's a day, it's the sort of stuff you would expect someone twenty years younger to be accumulating—skis, bicycles, baseball paraphernalia, golf clubs, a speedboat. No one has ever seen him use any of it.

Appetizer

Karen made a pea and cauliflower salad. It is our contribution to dinner with the Snyders.

"Just bring anything," Amy said.

"How about an appetizer or some sort of a salad?" Karen asked.

"A salad is fine."

The "fine" thing about this salad is that it is easy to make, but it looks hard.

Alchemists

While I don't sell insurance, the company I work for employs people who do. In the face of catastrophe we offer hope and salvation. We are alchemists. We turn fear into money.

Angry

Katherine Kramer has started getting angry in meetings. She has started doing this under the mistaken impression that if she acts like some of her male counterparts, she will be treated like them. This is not the case. Her anger is just annoying people she shouldn't be annoying and suggesting to some—who she should not be suggesting anything to—that she is headed for a nervous collapse.

Assorted

The subject line of the memo I wrote read simply: Assorted Issues.

Amuse

I don't know exactly why I wrote "Assorted Issues"— I was bored and frustrated I guess. It was a way of amusing myself, a way of avoiding the despair that sweeps over me regularly several times a day. It never occurred to me that anyone would read it.

Apologizing

Russell McGahan is a nice old man. He is my neighbor to the east. Like a lot of old men, he has a well-stocked store of regrets. One in particular that seems to come up often in conversation is the regret he feels at not having been a better father to his son. He is constantly apologizing. Russell doesn't feel he took sufficient interest in the boy when he was young. He says too often he was just tired—his work in the upper-middle echelons of the banking industry taking out most of what he had in him. I told Russell he shouldn't believe everything he reads—a father's presence in his son's life is not inevitably a blessing.

AC

It is to me what the heart-lung machine is to the surgeon: essential. Physically I can survive the summer without it; emotionally I cannot. If it breaks down, I break down.

Awkward

Most of the dreams I have are interesting only for the awkward outlandishness of their peculiarity, and most of the ones I am told—if interesting at all—are similarly interesting only for their strangeness, not for their profundity. I wish I could say I had a recurring one—I like what that would suggest about the complexity of my psyche—but I haven't yet, so I am inclined to doubt I ever will.

Awake

It's always difficult to imagine what is keeping Karen awake. She has so many things on her mind. While I am toying with some anesthetizing fantasy, she is worrying about her mother's health or her brothers—one of them between jobs, the other between marriages. Tonight I have the feeling it is one of her students.

We were talking about him at dinner. But maybe it is about me—the way I have been acting lately.

Astonishing

Karen, who notices everything there is to notice about me, finds it astonishing that Elizabeth (across the alley) doesn't seem to know whether her husband is right or left-handed. "I bet there was a time when she used to know," Karen says, shaking her head ever so slightly.

Act

I don't really seem to know how to act anymore. When I was younger, knowing didn't really seem to be a question—now, at some level, it always is.

Adopted

The Jenners over on Stimpson Street have just adopted their fourth underprivileged child. Like most of the neighbors, I respect them enormously—but like a few, I find myself also wondering exactly what it is they are trying to prove, and to whom.

Abnormality

Someday the doctor is going to find one. That is the day the compromising truly begins.

Afternoon

David May has been closed up in his office all afternoon working on the mysterious presentation he will be making tomorrow. A certifiably neurotic perfectionist, he worries about everything—so to save himself embarrassment, he prepares and prepares and prepares. He does this with an intensity the rest of us find peculiar and frightening.

Accident

Periodically I am stupefied by a sense that it is all just part of an infinitely vast, complex, ongoing accident. I can barely get up out of my chair and get myself another glass of wine.

B

Brother

I've never wished I had one, and I wonder why. They are supposed to be a good thing to have, but I can't really imagine it. Heather has one. He's fat and depressed and lies around the house all day watching television. I've never met him, but I don't like knowing he is there. I don't like the idea of him rummaging around in the refrigerator.

Breather

Boyd was gone for two weeks on vacation to who-knows-where. It was nice not to have him here. I didn't have to think about him at all. I didn't have to worry about running into him at the communal mail-boxes. I didn't have to see him washing his car or hear him out on the patio talking to one of his despicable buddies. Wouldn't it be wonderful if he just weren't here any more—ever?

Beaverton

The Snyders live in the suburbs—not just any suburb, but Beaverton—and not just in any part of Beaverton, but in the part located somewhere on or around, or at least within cursing distance, of Scholls Ferry Road. I remember reading a restaurant review a long time ago by a columnist who called himself Mr. Dishing-It-Out. I could have written it myself. Dishing-It-Out said that in the five years he had lived in Portland, he had been lost more often and more completely in Beaverton than in any other part of town. At first he thought it was just him, but an informal poll suggested otherwise. It seemed almost everyone had trouble with Beaverton. He said that unlike your average, angst-ridden French existentialist, he had never been able to take any pleasure in getting lost. He invariably found it more annoying than ennobling, which is why he was so much less than overwhelmingly enthusiastic about accepting his editors' malicious dare to survey this local labyrinth's gastronomic scene.

Anyway, the point is I avoid the area if I can. A quagmire of serpentine tangents, whimsical name changes, and deadends, it always makes me tense. As much as I like the Snyders, I feel certain I would like them more if they lived in a part of town I could understand.

Buick

Russell loves his dog, his television, and his Buick. He is the sort of man who has fond memories of the family vacation.

Babble

The memo, Assorted Issues, started out as an uncensored

commentary on company policies and procedures. For example, there were some remarks about the latest changes in our healthcare coverage. While our previous plan had come perilously close to being comprehensible, this new one did not. But even with the addition of yet another layer of confusion—pages of babble about something called a "deductible credit bank"—the powers-that-be failed, I think, to obscure the fact that we were now paying more and getting less. This is particularly true for the newly hired—but, of course, who cares about them.

Blank Verse

Karen is a teacher (high school English), and she is tireless in her efforts to educate me—mostly about relationships and life, but occasionally about the use of the semicolon or the virtues of blank verse. The clarity with which she sees certain things still astonishes me even after all this time.

Basketball

The company will occasionally offer us free tickets to the basketball game. They have some sort of financial arrangement with the team, which is this year what it is every year—mediocre. Even if I liked basketball, these are not the guys I would want to watch play it.

Blunt

I was encouraged by the bluntness of Frank McDonald's comments the other day on the general state of a long-running program here (involving telephone sales) that has always bothered me. I recently wrote a memo on one of the subprograms involved. It was a slight, peculiar thing as memos go and of virtually no interest to the middle managers who Frank had so gracefully excoriated. I don't know why I never thought of sending him a copy. I guess it's because I'm just not very good at this sort of thing.

Bought

Karen bought some expensive new sheets last week, and we have been sleeping in a set of them for a few days now. I'm still distracted nightly by the silkiness of their texture and amazed that I can feel so strongly about the simple pleasure they provide. New sheets—they are way up there in the hierarchy of good things: like an unexpected piece of peach pie or a new episode of the *Sopranos*. New sheets—I never would have thought I could have cared.

Boldness

The people in David May's meeting are as serious about it as he is. Dressed in their nice but not-too-nice suits, differentiated only by the length of their sideburns and the boldness of their ties, you can see how deeply pleased they are with themselves to be there. It is not this particular meeting, but this kind of meeting that excites them—a meeting with important people and presentations. It makes them feel part of something valuable and big.

Baffling

If whatever is keeping Karen awake keeps keeping her awake, she will get up and wander down the hall to the guest room where we have a loveseat and a lamp. She will read for a while—probably something about Africa. This baffling continent has been a long-time obsession of hers. She is attracted to the mystery, the adventure, the bravery of the place.

Bumbler

There was an announcement made today that Thomas Brier, one of our departmental directors, is retiring. I don't think anyone is going to be sorry to see him go. The job was given to him years ago as a favor—payback for services his father rendered to one of the more significant members of our senior command. An autocratic, unreflective bumbler, he has turned out to be pretty much the disaster everyone predicted.

C

Character

Paul Drabble is one. He is my father's age. He has black hair that he combs back on the sides in a fanciful fashion. At first glance he looks normal enough, but if you peer into his eyes you can tell there are unusual things going on in his head. When you listen to him speak it is like listening to someone doing a translation—instead of from German to English, it is from odd to ordinary. I once played doctor with his daughter—a horsey girl named Anne.

Congestion

"I hate driving around over here."

"I know," Karen said, running through a list of other places I had expressed similar feelings about. She had a point. There are lots of places I don't want to go—places I go to far less frequently than I might if getting to them or around in them was easier, more straightforward. Trial by confusion or traffic congestion is not the best way for me to start an adventure. I prefer places I know I can get to efficiently, places that will leave me with more of what I will need for the afternoon or evening ahead.

Considerably

Once I'm stressed by a situation it takes me forever to get unstressed—by which time it is almost always too late because I've been less than my best (sometimes considerably less) and to one degree or another have damaged our outing.

Censorious

The Snyders are not nearly as opinionated as Karen and me. They have strong feelings about their family—but philosophically, politically, culturally, we feel much more censorious.

Cannon Beach

It is one of my favorite places. I'm supposed to hate it—not because it is touristy but because it is a particular type of touristy, which is an upscale type, a type that is distinctly different from the regular tacky type of other beach towns. (Like Seaside, for instance, which one is not necessarily expected to like, but is certainly not expected to hate with anything like the special sanctimony reserved for CB.) I like it because it's small, compact, and has a wonderful beach. I like it because of the Lazy Susan Cafe where we eat breakfast every morning—waffles with sliced pears and lemon sauce. And then there's the bookstore that was more impressive when John owned it (before he built on the back room), but is still better than okay.

Courageous

Russell worries a lot about being a decent person. (It's one of the most decent things about him.) He is tormented by the way he feels about Mrs. Lurie down the street. Mrs. Lurie is in a wheelchair, the consequence of an automobile accident many years ago. He finds it a bit depressing to watch her be so unrelentingly courageous.

Commentary

If the memo Assorted Issues started out as an uncensored commentary on company policies and procedures, it evolved into one on the characters who populate every nook and cranny of this place. They are not flashy characters in the Hollywood, high-concept sense—that is, no one as far as I know has superpowers, a connection to organized crime, or a murdered daughter for whom they are secretly seeking revenge—but they are, in many cases, ardent.

Cut Off

I feel most distinctly an outsider when it comes to certain things—like wanting to be talked to or about. I have no interest in either, so I am cut off from what percentage of the population?

Clocks

I have three of them on my nightstand. The alarms are set to go off one after the other. Each is louder than the one before because it takes a lot to get me up after I've gone to sleep. The first alarm to go off is the least effective. I don't really need it, but I like the clock because in addition to telling me the time, it tells me the temperature. Next is the dressy brass one. Finally, there is a stubby little siren-like thing. They are all battery-operated. I don't want to be thrown off schedule by some unanticipated power outage.

Control

The woman at the cash register asked me whether I wanted my groceries loaded into paper or plastic bags. Paper. It was a small choice, but I was happy to make it. One should control what they can because what they can't is everywhere and always.

Council

I had lunch with David Joyce at a place called The Vat. We spent most of the hour talking about the latest city council debacle—the almost criminally clumsy attempt to rename a city street after union organizer Cesar Chavez. We agreed that sometimes the sheer ineptitude of these guys could take your breath away. When you watched something simple like this being handled so poorly in public, you could only imagine what happened behind closed doors with something complex.

Conscientious

Karen has an office upstairs, but she prefers to work at the kitchen table. Night after night you will find her there sitting on the edge of her chair sipping a cup of tea and grading her way through the latest pile of student essays, undaunted by the logic, the grammar, the vocabulary, the deep-seated lack of interest. Conscientious to a fault, she scribbles her kind corrections and her carefully worded criticisms in a crazy cacographic scrawl up one margin and down the other.

Church

I am at a point in my life when I cannot or will not read, watch, or listen to anything that begins with a scene in a church or from a dream.

Careful

I've never really been careful about what I say, and I've never been able to decide whether I should be or not. I am sure there have been times when it would have been nicer or wiser if I had been, but I don't know if there has ever been a time when it would have been something I should have done as a matter of principle.

Corner

Over the years I have worked myself into a snug little corner here. As much as possible, I try to stay out of everyone's way and hope to be left alone. Of course, one can be only marginally successful at this sort of thing. At least once a month I end up on the managerial map and am drafted to work on projects for which I have neither the temperament nor training.

Calliope

One of four words Karen habitually mispronounced in grade school. The others were "aluminum," "hierarchical," and "asterisk."

Comic Books

In an office this size you would expect somebody to be trying to write a screenplay, but nobody is. It just isn't that sort of crowd. The closest thing we have to a creative type is Paul Hamilton, an intern in accounting whose mental and emotional development was arrested somewhere near the onset of adolescence. According to those in the know—the pencil-lickers he exchanges emails with--he is working on a series of science-fiction comic books.

Chihuahua

I have never been able to understand the point of one. It's not a hamster, and it's not really a dog. Perhaps the attraction is related to the childhood fantasy of having a toy come to life.

Cough

I think it was the word "entrepreneurial" that got wrapped around David May's tonsils. It started him coughing. Once he started, it didn't seem like he could stop. When he did stop, it was too late—the mood was mangled.

Chicken

I saw one killed when I was very young. I must have

gotten over it—I mean, look what I had for dinner last night. Still, on some level I think this messy, matter-of-fact beheading changed me. It was a real, three-dimensional barbarity I could understand—an introduction to a world I was not really ready to know existed.

D

Dog

Karen wants one and I don't. I can barely take care of myself, how am I going to take care of a dog. Karen says she will take care of it and I'm sure she will, but she can't take care of it all the time, which means I'll have to take care of it some, and I don't want to. If I have time to take care of a dog, then I have time to do something else, and if I have time to do something else, I'd rather be doing it because that something else could be *the* something else that makes all the difference.

Dabbler

I am one in the visual arts. I once played with painting, but I had no talent for it so moved over to photography. The camera is a crutch for people like me—people who can't paint. I may not be very good with it, but I'm better than most of the people here at the office—Kathryn Perlich, for example, or Jessica Myers, both of whom seem to think they know what they are doing.

Desperate

Saw Joseph Farrell the other day and the phrase

"desperate for recognition" popped into my head. I have no idea where it came from—I probably read it somewhere. Wherever it came from, it describes Farrell perfectly—you sense it in everything he does around here, from the way he dresses to the way he speaks to the people he chooses to be seen standing next to. Recognition is nice enough, but it doesn't really matter to me the way it probably should. This relative indifference to it is a symptom of something. What? Well, about that I'm sure there are innumerable theories.

Difficult

We wanted our contribution to this evening's dinner to be good and at least look like something that was difficult to prepare because we wanted the Snyders to feel flattered, to assume we had made an investment. We wanted them to feel flattered because we were feeling guilty. We liked the Snyders—living off Scholls Ferry Road or not—but we had not been as good a friends to them as we should lately. We hadn't been as good a friends to them as we should because (for the usual reasons—mostly having to do with me) we hadn't been as good a friends as we should to anyone.

The Snyders are, by our standards anyway, exceptionally social people. We would estimate they had three or four sets of friends they liked better than us, and three or four sets they liked less. We had the feeling that because we had been negligent lately the Randalls—the couple just below us in this hierarchy of friendly estimation—had supplanted us in the Snyders' affections. We hoped with this difficult-looking salad, with what it said about how much we valued the relationship, we might recover our former position in their regard.

Dumbfounding

Russell is a religious man, but not obnoxiously so (like Mike Farmer, for instance). His belief is, I think, a cautious one. He does not presume to know or prescribe. Still, he is comfortable with the idea of an afterlife—feels certain of it in a way I envy but ultimately find dumbfounding. The subject keeps coming up because Russell keeps losing friends. He visits those left behind. It never gets any easier. He can never find the right thing to say (or a better thing to say) than what he does—which is simply that he is sorry and that he knows how hard it must be.

Delusion

I have a philosophical reverence for truth and a psychological one for delusion—which puts me in something of a bind. I may want to believe only things that are true and still need to believe those that are not. I have a feeling—which I try to regularly ignore—that the only thing standing between me and despair are some wispy figments of my imagination.

Downsizing

It has been going on for a while now—the company, like most in this industry, has been downsizing. I used to share this office with Rebecca Brown. She is no longer here. It has become a lonelier, more desolate place without her, but there have been compensations. For instance, I got Rebecca's tape dispenser, a sleek black desk model made of heavy metal that is much nicer than that pathetic plastic thing I used to have. And—more importantly—I am no longer obligated to decorate the place for Halloween and Christmas.

Down The Hall

The first thing I do when I wake up in the morning is try to ignore my mood. This is followed by my walking down the hall to give Karen a kiss on the forehead. (No kissing on the lips—I haven't brushed my teeth yet.) Karen gets up earlier than I do and perfects herself in the guest bath. After the kiss on the forehead, I wander off to find my pants.

Decorating

In general when it comes to decorating the house, I know what to buy; Karen knows where to put it.

Differences

We share so many things that our differences come as a surprise to some. For instance: Karen likes light; I like dark. She likes hot hotsauce; I like mild or medium. She likes crowded stores; I like empty ones. She likes summer; I like winter. She likes the volume turned up; I like it turned down. She likes flat land; I like mountains. She likes sofas; I like chairs. She likes to be in the middle of things; I like to be on the distant periphery. She likes to be outside; I like to be in. She is always late; I am always early.

Day

How was my day? I'm trying not to remember.

Division

The division between the new people just coming in and those of us who have been around for a while seems to have become more marked in the past few years. We look at these new arrivals—the brightness in their faces, the sharp creases of their collars—and we wonder just what it is they think they are going to end up doing here. We wonder where they get their ideas about what is in store for them.

Delightful

Every other semester it seems there is a student who tries especially hard to get Karen's attention. This semester it is a young man named Brian Veronski. He has been doing his best to seem delightful. He wants to talk to Karen about extra work for special credit.

Doing

It seems that as you go along you start having to do more and more things you don't want to do until finally you reach a point where you are doing almost nothing else.

Demonstrative

Karen is a physically demonstrative speaker—which means at dinner things are always getting knocked over.

Duo

David May and Kevin Sharp were brought in almost a year ago to do something—or at least May was. He brought Sharp with him. What they were supposed to do isn't exactly clear—something different from whatever it is that was being done because whatever it was that was being done had been being done the way it was for a long time and everyone was sure a change must be needed. Nothing really came of the effort, but certain people in certain offices were convinced this dynamic duo should be kept on in a sort of adjunct capacity—the idea being that at some point (nobody knew exactly what point) they were going to be exactly what was needed somewhere.

Docile

Darren Verde is one of the people rumored to be in the running for Brier's job. I find that hard to believe--mainly for physiognominal reasons. A short, docile man with flapping ears and a large, peculiar, potato-shaped head, he looks like a garden gnome gone wrong. He would be a sort of sight-gag on ceremonial occasions—not something you would expect our image-conscious elite to countenance.

Dental

We could have bought another car with the money we have spent on Karen's dental work.

E

Eschatology

Like most biology professors, my grandfather was inordinately fond of end-of-the-world-as-we-know-it theories. He tinkered obsessively with half a dozen of them—everything from pandemic viral infections to atmospheric aberrations that interfered with the basic processes of photosynthesis. He shared them all with me and, as a consequence, seriously undermined my pint-sized faith in the idea that there was going to be a tomorrow.

Eroticism

There are those who like to suggest it is something of an achievement to infuse a work with erotic charge—a photograph, a painting, a novel, a movie, a remark. It isn't. Given the nature of the animal, nothing could be easier. Eroticism can be applauded, of course, but we shouldn't pretend producing it is difficult.

Extraordinary

The Snyders are gourmets. They are not fussy about it, but they are serious—serious enough to prepare something scrumptious and different every time, serious enough to put pressure on anyone contributing to an evening's dinner. Karen and I have only a passing familiarity with the kitchen. We would like to get more involved, but we just haven't had the time. We are a long way from the Snyders and the Lanphears (the couple we believe to be just above us on the Snyder's ladder of love). We had dinner with both of them not long ago. It was extraordinary. There was cream of sorrel soup, stuffed halibut steaks, and apricot pie. And, to tell you the truth, a little too much talk about the production of it all. Listening to them was like listening to people speaking a foreign language. There were disquisitions on fennel seed, olive oil, and balsamic vinegar. A lot of time was spent talking about the pros and cons of decorating a dinner ham—time Karen and I (who had enjoyed the sorrel soup, stuffed halibut steaks, and apricot pie very much) would rather have spent talking about the Tuckers, a couple we all knew who were involved in a lawsuit with some Hollywood movie people over the damage done to their home during the filming of yet another lousy movie made here last summer.

Edge

When I shave I listen to the radio (NPR—how else am I going to keep up with what's going on in Pakistan?). I've given up trying to know what I look like. I thought I had a rough idea until I got my new driver's license. That picture—which I assume to be as unbiased a thing as that benighted bureaucracy can produce—has caused me to reassess all sorts of things:

for instance, the general feeling I have about how long I will live. The general feeling I used to have was that I would be alive about as long as I had been alive. Obviously that is not true. What I see when I look at that picture is someone on the edge—someone on the edge of the edge. Apparently I am not going to have to do all that planning for the future I thought I was going to have to do because it seems the future—or my future—is only about 60% of what I had been subconsciously supposing it to be.

Expropriation

Carol Delgado from advertising services has expropriated the best table in the lunchroom for a group of automatonamous Bible studiers.

Exotic

I remember the first time I saw Karen. I was sitting in a restaurant with my friend, a homosexual cinemaphile by the name of Nicholas Anzio. Karen walked in with three other girls. Nick pointed her out. "She's sort of exotic looking don't you think?" I turned. For Nick it was normally a matter of principle to overstate the case, but, in this instance, with "exotic" he did not so much overstate it as simply misidentify it. The emphasis in "exotic" is on an unusualness that is foreign. There was nothing foreign about Karen. Tan, long brown hair, wearing a tight, short-sleeved yellow sweater—what was unusual was her prettiness. It was a rare, singular, substantive sort.

Expected

Karen's conference with Brian went pretty much as expected—Brian trying to appear to be a sincerely committed young man mature beyond his years; Karen trying to appear teacherly and fair. For special credit they agreed on a ten-page report. Karen recommended what, on these occasions, she always recommends—the quintessential beginners' book for boys: Ernest Hemingway's *The Old Man and the Sea*.

Elude

The things that go on in some people's minds amaze me—they also frequently bore me, but more often than not they simply elude me.

Ex

Jim Manning, who is my age, is living the bachelor life out of a small condo in the Pearl district. He was divorced four years ago. His ex-wife remarried and moved to Chicago. His daughter moved there too. Right now he is seeing someone named Jennifer, but he won't be for long. She has started to call him late at night.

Equanimity

I can't decide if it would have been a good thing or a bad thing to have been Russell's son. His equanimity and understanding would have been unassailable and consequently either depressing, infuriating, or both.

Everything

Something ended when I married Karen, and something else began. The something that began has been everything—if it hadn't been, the something that ended would have seemed nothing but a pointless torture.

Everyone

John Kiessling is the departmental party boy. He thinks it's just the thing to wake up feeling like shit, having spent the night abusing substances—alcohol, mostly—at the new place everyone is talking about as being the new place everyone is talking about. We used to have more like him—guys who sought to distinguish themselves through heroic acts of dissipation, guys who found something fascinating about the latest in poseurs—people with things shaved, painted, or pierced; people who could spend the night talking about the price of their tattoos—but they have mostly disappeared like the fashions they chased, and now it is pretty much just John.

Exhausted

In some ways it's a good thing I'm perpetually exhausted. The only reason I'm not a bigger, more troublesome mess is that I simply don't have the energy to be.

F

Father

Mine is a tax accountant by day and an expert on the Kennedy assassination by night. He has written several highly respected articles on the subject—his forte being the debunking of crackpot conspiracy theories. While we have our differences, we share a suspicion of mystery. We fear the uses to which a belief in it can be put.

Faces

We were going through a phase where we were being neglectful of everyone, but I think we were being a little more neglectful of the Snyders than of our other friends. One of the reasons was the Snyders' children: Cynthia and Jeffrey. They are probably no worse than the children we would have had, had we had children, but their parents, who are very much up on all of the latest childrearing techniques (Amy being a psychotherapist), have been a little too successful in their efforts to promote self-esteem. Visiting the Snyders invariably means an evening that begins with an hour or so of their children's company. At some point— while being shown the latest watercolor, or listening to some charming song just learned in school—we always find ourselves struggling to keep the misery off our faces and out of our voices.

Farmer

I don't know if Russell was always a mutterer, but he certainly is one now. Being on his own hasn't helped. Funny, I can't really decide how I feel about it. It seems annoying and endearing at the same time. He once told me that he wished he had been a wheat farmer.

Few Days Off

I get up as late as I can so there is no time for breakfast before I leave the house. Breakfast is at my desk. It usually consists of yogurt, a granola bar, and coffee. On weekends breakfast is a bowl of cereal with a banana cut up in it, and on special occasions—like when we are taking a few days off and going to the beach—it's the Hands On Café where there is always something innovative and wonderful.

Familiar

There is that familiar pause at the door every morning just before I walk into the building—that moment when I take my last breath of cool outside air and head into the canned, fluorescently lit air of the office. It feels like I am boarding some sort of psychic submarine. The hatch is sealed behind me, and shortly I will be submerged.

Functions

The company has two obligatory social functions a year—a Christmas party and in June or July a departmental barbecue. We go, of course, but we don't stay long and we do our best to avoid Doug Carr. Doug is one of those Jekyll-and-Hyde characters—nice enough in his daily life, but belligerent when he drinks. Invariably he corners Karen and wants to argue. Usually he wants to argue about the state of education these days. He doesn't really know anything about the state of education these days, but he knows Karen is a teacher and he wants to tell her how much he dislikes the way teachers do almost everything.

Fortitude

I don't know that I ever thought I really had any, but, as of late, I know for certain that I don't.

Faint

I have never known anyone who has fainted nor have I ever come close to fainting myself. It strikes me as a sort of suspicious thing to do.

Foreign

I don't speak any foreign languages. It seems to me if I had been brought up right I should be able to speak at least one. I have just a smidgen of French that I learned for our vacation a few years ago, but it was really Karen who got us around, who unconfused the confusion between the sound-alike words for "traffic light" (*feu*) and "flower" (*fleur*) so we knew exactly where to turn right—at the signal, not at the garden. It was Karen with her sincere efforts who got us treated generously almost everywhere.

Forms

I've just noticed how many I have sitting on my desk at the moment—five. Every day I find them laying here waiting to be filled in by me, and every day that is exactly what I do. My hand flies around the page mechanically without hesitation, checking this and that off; initialing and dating where required—upper left, lower right, dead center. Occasionally a comment is called for.

Fast

Jason Ferris is the office speed-walker. No matter how fast you might be going down the hall, it is not fast enough for him. He is always right behind you or trying to squeeze past. The not-so-subliminal message he invariably seeks to send is that he is on a mission—not just any old mission, but one that is vital and important (and you, my sad, dawdling friend, are not).

Fit In

I don't know exactly when I lost my desire to fit in. I remember having it in grade school. I don't remember having it in college.

Fun

Nancy Wright is John Kiessling's immediate supervisor. He doesn't particularly like her. She represents funlessness and responsibility. Nancy, for her part, doesn't much care for Kiessling. Troublesome, a little on the smug side, not very productive—keeping on top of him takes up more of her time than she would like. She would get rid of him if she could, but because he reminds Robert Carlton, her supervisor, of what he likes to think of as his own rascally younger self, he has been given one chance after another.

First

There are things I know that don't seem to be of any help to me at all. You would think I might be the first person to benefit, but I'm not. It doesn't seem I am the second, third, fourth, or fifth either.

Fingernails

It wasn't that long ago that Karen stopped biting hers—four or five years at most.

Future

Apparently it cannot be predicted.

G

Glasses

When I was nine I hypnotized myself staring at the stars. I wasn't able to snap out of it so I was taken to see a man who may or may not have been a psychologist. All I really remember about him are his glasses—the lenses were thick and tinted an eerie aquarium green.

Gingersnaps

I am addicted to them. I eat two boxes a week and have for I don't know how many years. While there are some dubious medical claims made for ginger by the usual naturopathic nutters, I can't believe they are good for me in this quantity. I wonder which of my obscurer organs has been most adversely affected.

Gratuitous

Steven Grieg, my boss's boss, stopped by my desk this afternoon to drop off a gratuitous remark about my job performance. He asked me if I remembered a report so-and-so had asked me for a couple of days ago—a report I had looked for and eventually said did not exist. I remembered it. Well, it seems so-and-so found this report himself yesterday. Of course later when I had time, I looked into it. I discovered the report so-and-so had found was not exactly the one he had asked me for. The one he had asked me for contained several parameters that turned out not to be in the report he actually wanted. As a consequence, my computer searches had been fruitless. Why did Grieg go out of his way to stop by and suggest I was not doing a very good job? Is it some sort of temperamental inclination to be disapproving? Perhaps. But I think it's more than that. I think it's personal. I think Grieg is hostile toward me for reasons that flatter neither of us.

Gratifying

We were in the car on the way to the Snyders when Karen brought up the subject of our first meeting. There is something that we all liked about this story because every few years we would retell it to one another at a celebration dinner. It started with Karen meeting Charles. Charles owned an electronics store that sold expensive state-of-the-art audio and video equipment. It was in a part of town I understood geographically, but not economically—an enclave swarming with young people who couldn't possibly afford to live there, but did. Karen was looking for something special for her father's seventieth birthday, and Charles found it for her. He was patient, informative, and knew just the right piece of gear—a whatchamacallit that turned out to be, gratifyingly enough, just exactly what her father had wanted. She and Charles hit it off, and Karen, who was always after one sort of thing or another for her office, for here, for someone in the family, started dropping by occasionally. For instance, she bought the system I was just listening to the people from NPR on.

Good Terms

Russell's was an inexplicably decorous, not-unhappy, late-in-life divorce. Everyone seems to have remained on remarkably good terms with one another. This is in large part due to the sanguinity of his temperament.

Germs

I try not to pay any attention to them because I know if I did I would probably never be able to stop. I would devolve—quickly I'm sure—into one of those obsessive hand-washers who won't touch anything that hasn't been disinfected or wrapped in plastic.

Gravel

The drive to work has recently gotten better because the city has repaved a section of the road I use. It was an absolutely terrible piece of highway with potholes, protruding manhole covers, and all sorts of gravel patches. It loosened my teeth every morning and who knows how many nuts and bolts on the car. I was always expecting something to fall off one or the other of us. It took five years to get it done, but it was worth it. I don't really get here any faster, but I do get here a little less rattled.

Garrulous

It surprises me every morning to see so many people look so wide awake and fresh—like this is the optimum hour of the day for them. They are full of a garrulous energy—full of hope and hellos. I don't really have an optimal hour here—my optimal hour is at home late at night. Here it is a matter of resigning myself to the situation. It can take me half-a-day to get into the flow that will ultimately sweep me on to quitting time.

Gadgets

Our electronic gadgets are rebelling against us. Karen's cell phone has started to malfunction, and so has her computer. The main outlet for our land-line went dead, the burglar alarm stopped working, and some sensor in the car has started giving us an erroneous trouble message. (We have checked the fuel cap several times—it's fine.) All this in the last two days.

Greetings

Some of the stores downtown have started standing employees at their entrances to greet me when I walk in. Just what my day needs—one more meaningless exchange with a complete stranger.

Groups

This place is divided—but not evenly—between those who are living the happiest part of their life here and those who are living that part of their life somewhere else. The former group, with their gratitudes and attitudes, make it a better, pleasanter place for the latter—while the latter, with their complaints and their detachment, offer the former little or nothing.

Guitar

Jim Hammond and Jeff Merrick are always invited to these sorts of things: Jim because he does card tricks, Jeff because he plays the guitar.

Grapevine

Confirmed through the venerable grapevine, the field of candidates for the Director's job seems to have been narrowed to two: the trusty, helmet-haired Helen Cooper and the up-and-coming, eloquently earnest Brian O'Donnell.

H

Hearing

I have exceptional hearing so I rely on earplugs most of the day. I wear them when Patrick, the guy in the office next to me, is playing his hideous radio or being visited by his friend Mary who sounds like a 150-pound macaw. I wear them in the evening at home when I read, when I draw, when I sleep. I never go anywhere without a pair because I never know when I am going to need to shut something out. The ones I am using now are orange and made of silicon. They are the highest-rated reusable earplugs currently made anywhere in the world. It says so on the box.

Haystack Rock

It is the clichéd, iconic image of the Oregon coast. How many photographs have I taken of it?—two or three dozen a year for the past twenty years. I just can't not take a picture of it when I'm there. I don't have the strength of character.

Hobby

Hating Boyd seems to have become something of a hobby.

However

When Karen found out Charles was married to a psychotherapist, we tried not to hold it against him. We invited them for dinner at our place. There was a storm that night that knocked out the electricity in our neighborhood, so we were not able to cook. When they arrived we had nothing to eat. We did, however, have some candles and several bottles of wine.

Headache

Black-and-white photography or color—the discussion of the pros and cons gives me a headache. I am reluctant to admit it, but as a work of art—or as something as close to a work of art as a photograph can be—I much prefer black-and-white. Of course I don't take any black-and-white pictures myself.

Handy

One of the things I like about Russell is that he is hardly handy at all. He looks like someone who would be, but he isn't. He never had an interest in that sort of thing— nothing beyond the most elementary, that is.

Hardboiled

When I was done playing with Assorted Issues I sent a copy to my friend Gail, one of the few people here who I knew would get the jokes. What I didn't know at the time was that Gail was on vacation. Roberta Forsythe, a conscienceless, hardboiled conservative with a taste for dirty tricks, was covering her desk.

She found the memo, read it, and made copies. Now they seem to be floating around everywhere.

High Opinion

Russell's ex-wife remarried several years ago. His children seem to have a high opinion of the man, who is apparently from Ireland and has a beard.

Habit

There is always a little drama involved in pulling into my parking lot. I have to drive up a narrow ramp to a remote-controlled gate. Because of the angles and certain obstructions, I cannot see if there is a car exiting down the ramp until I make the turn onto it. If there is a car coming down the ramp I have to back out into a moderately busy two-way street to let it out. (Backing up the ramp and into the parking structure is possible, but tricky and not advisable.) I always dread being forced into this little reverse maneuver. It's a necessary courtesy that I habitually resent.

Harder

My day begins with returning calls, with answering inquiries left on my phone. These inquiries have a tendency to be devastatingly repetitive. It gets harder and harder throughout the day (throughout the week, throughout the month, throughout the year) to fake an interest in them—harder and harder to sound properly enthusiastic.

Happen

You would think eventually one would have to reach a point where they would give up trying to find an explanation for the world in which the things that happen happen—but apparently not. Some people can just go on asking forever. I don't think I'm one of them.

Halfway

There is a town in Oregon called Halfway. Karen and I were going to visit, but it was a long drive. We got only halfway to Halfway when we turned around. We knew that philosophically it was possible we could never get there (see Zeno). Since we didn't really have any good reason to do it geographically, we decided to see Hamley's instead—the famous Western shop in Pendleton where they make saddles right there in front of you.

Hospital

As phobic as I am of airports, I am even more so of hospitals—the light, the chilled air, the smell, the powder-blue curtains on their metal hooks. Every bed in every room is filled—or was filled just an hour ago—with a story so sad that to simply imagine it is to feel yourself eviscerated.

Halloween

I don't know if it's a national phenomenon, but here it seems to be getting more popular with adults every year. Everyone, it seems, wants to get dressed up in some sort of elaborate costume—they want to be pirates, gorillas, important figures from history. Neither Karen nor I have converted—we still think of it as a holiday for kids. We remember how important a quality piece of candy was to us so when the time comes, we pass out only the best name-brand stuff.

Hall

Who do I least want to look up and see coming down that hall? Predictably enough, I'd have to say Harris.

Hangover

In the morning John Kiessling likes to pretend everything is either too loud or too bright for him. He seems to think we will be impressed by his hangover, that we will conclude there is something magnificent about him.

Horses

Karen is afraid of horses—they are so large and unfathomable. She finds them beautiful, but she doesn't think that is really a reason to have anything to do with them. Somehow as a child I seem to have had them in my life at regular intervals. I have fed them, washed them, ridden them bareback, and been bitten by them. Alhough it has faded, you can still see the crescent-shaped scar on my shoulder if you look carefully.

History

I hate going to a new doctor. I hate it for a lot of reasons. For instance, I hate being obliged to fill out yet another medical history form. Is there a more depressing document...?

Scarlet Fever?

No.

Meningitis?

No.

Tuberculosis?

No.

Asthma?

No.

Anemia?

No.

Diabetes?

No

Pleurisy?

No.

Hepatitis?

No.

Hives?

No.

Kidney disease?

No.

Healthwise, I've been very lucky, there's no doubt about it. But if from the beginning until now it has been no, no, no, no, what is it going to be from now until the end? What I am looking at when I am looking at one of these things is not my medical past but my medical future. It's dispiriting, to say the least.

Here are a few choice selections from the menu of things I have to look forward to:
High blood pressure,
Hemorrhoids,
Cancer,
Bladder infections,
Bronchitis,
Arthritis,
Heart disease,
Gout,
Back trouble,
Emphysema,
Gallbladder disease,
Varicose veins,
Hernia,
Loss of hearing,
Eye pain,
Nosebleeds,
Sore gums,
Coughing,
Swelling ankles,
Difficulty swallowing,
Nausea,
Muscle cramps,
Dizziness,
Change in bowel habits.

Housecleaning

Karen and I have divided the housecleaning duties down the middle—she does sinks, toilets, and various countertops while I do all of the floors and the general dusting. If one or the other of us has a complaint about the way one thing or the other is being done, well then they are certainly welcome to do it themselves.

Haircut

I'm lucky if I get one good haircut a year. It's not Bob's fault—it's the tricky cowlicks and my oddly shaped head.

I

Isolation

There are people who believe I need to be rescued from it. I suppose it's no surprise that I'm not one of them.

Investing

The Snyders' table had been set in advance. There was something slightly off-putting about the flawless matching of this with that. The plates—mauve with blue accents—were ostentatiously tasteful. They looked and felt expensive. They were the sort of plates people who entertained a lot more than we did felt comfortable investing in.

Illusion

The power of the black-and-white photograph is in the drama, and the drama is in the information not provided, the thing not said. The world exists in color. To ignore this, to embrace the artificial ignorance of black-and-white, is a provocative act and should be viewed with suspicion. There is depth, and there is the illusion of depth. Sometimes they are the same thing. Usually they are not.

Invitation

My name is on the memo. People will know who I am or think they know who I am, and they will start approaching me about this and that. They will not pick up on the subtextural insinuations that clearly suggest it was a game of solitaire and not some invitation to get in touch.

Industry Standards

Russell was forced into early retirement by mergers and acquisitions. The banking company he worked for was bought by somebody who was bought by somebody who was bought by somebody who already had several somebodys like Russell on the payroll, so they cut him loose with a pat on the back, some well-dones, and a severance package that was considered generous by industry standards.

Immunize

My first break is at 9:30 a.m. I spend it in the second-floor lunchroom with a book. I usually try to find a place near one of the windows. Right now I am re-reading Laurence Sterne's *Tristram Shandy*. I haven't looked at it since college. Sterne's peculiar, prolix playfulness invariably lifts my spirits. The hope is that a few pages will provide a sort of immunization—one that will last until my next break, which is for lunch.

Insufficient

Russell's older brother died last year. His name was Anthony. He taught Latin at the University of Somewhere. He was a scholarly person, the sort we used to honor before we came to fear that ultimately there was no point to knowing—that wisdom was a chimera and knowledge of consequence only insofar as it provided us with a means of distracting ourselves not from questions that were unanswerable, but from answers we knew to be woefully insufficient.

Ill

Karen and I have very different styles of being ill. Karen wants her mother or some sort of surrogate, and I want to be left alone. I envy her. She can be comforted; I cannot. Sympathy and concern make her feel better—for me it is only time and antibiotics that can do that.

Insane

I don't think Karen ever really worries about going insane. There is no family history—I mean there are some borderline cases, but no one you would call certifiable although she has an uncle who may be approaching. With age he seems to be getting scarier in his political beliefs and in the faith he puts in his ability to spot the investment scams he regularly exposes himself to as he seeks stranger and stranger ways of doubling, tripling, or quadrupling his retirement savings. She would miss me if I died, but she would survive. I'm not sure I can say the same. Just as I have never been able to believe that God exists, I would never be able to believe that Karen didn't—as a consequence, I can't imagine anything other than a babbling descent down the rabbit-hole into the waxed-hall depths of some idyllically named institution.

Infrastructure

Sometimes it seems everything happens at once—other times nothing seems to happen ever. Excitement and boredom—like heating and freezing, they play havoc with the integrity of one's infrastructure.

Interlocutor

I wish I could say I preferred one or the other—to feel something or know something. It would help me explain myself to the Grand Interlocutor—that weevil of the wee hours.

Itch

As a rule I am not an itchy person. Karen, on the other hand, seems to always have something that needs scratching. In some cases, it's several somethings.

Important

I would like to say that if a thing seems important to me, it is—but I know better. I know there are things that seem important to me that are not important to anyone else, and if I want to make the case for them, it will have to be a general one—something about the allowances one must make for the transforming power of unique experience in individual lives.

Illuminating

It was an illuminating thing to read the bio on the back of her book. A supposedly reluctant celebrity, she tells us not only where she was born but when; then she goes on to mention the schools she went to but did not graduate from. They were famous schools. It's as if she doesn't think the work itself is enough to convince us that she is smart and special—we have to hear about her semesters at Harvard (or was it Oxford).

Ida

If I have a formidable fondness for gingersnaps, I would say I have an even stronger one for pumpkin pie. No matter how cheap, rubbery, or ill- conceived— I have never had a piece I didn't like if it had a little whipped cream on it. The two best pumpkin pies I have ever had were from Jacaiva's Bakery and from Cal and Sue's Aunt Ida. Cal and Sue's Aunt Ida didn't actually make the pie I'm talking about: Cal and Sue did using her recipe. Jacaiva's we buy at Zupan's every year for Thanksgiving. Karen—generous to a fault— always lets me have at least half of her share.

Interest

There seems to be a lot of interest in the competition between Helen Cooper and Brian O'Donnell for Brier's old job. In fact, there is an office pool. Cooper—who seems to be the favorite—has experience and knows how to get things done; O'Donnell is young and has new ideas. There has been a lot of talk about the way they have started behaving civilly toward one another as of late. Everyone is wondering what it means. Some think it means O'Donnell is considering a position as Cooper's second-in-command, but Helen already has a second-in-command—big-nosed Bill Molina—and it doesn't seem likely to those in-the-know that she would dump him for O'Donnell. There has been lots of talk about who is supporting who and why and what that support will mean if one or the other of them gets the job. As for the new tone of their interdepartmental interaction, it is all about body language: who put their hand on whose shoulder, who leaned forward with a welcoming smile, who laughed at whose jokes. And then there is the behind-the-scenes stuff to which one or the other or both of them may or may not be responding. What did she say about what he said about what she said, and what did he say about what she said about what he said, and what did their saying what they said about what they said really say, and who did it say it to?

Imposing

Kurt Litterman likes to sit up very straight in his chair. He thinks it makes him look taller, more imposing, more alert. It doesn't really work—it just makes him look like somebody who has some sort of back problem. Listening to him meander through a memo is like listening to someone in high school give their geography report—except here you have to look interested.

If

Kiessling likes to not be where he should be when he should be. It is his way of marking his territory, of declaring his rights as a rebel. Of course, when he does appear, he always wants to know if Nancy Wright has been looking for him.

Inner

So much of the time it is this inner life of mine that seems actual and this actual one that seems an imposition.

J

Jealous

I am sure I am more so than I know, but she has never given me reason to find out. I've grown sort of accustomed to this certainty over time, but in the beginning it amazed me that she did not seem to realize how much more she deserved.

Jaunty

Russell moved to the coast. He bought a little place near Manzanita. He met the neighbors. Most were like himself—jaunty retirees with not enough to do. They were continually asking him to drop in. One of the things I have always liked about Russell is that he is not one of those people who is much for dropping in. Neither is he one who is much for being dropped in on.

Jumpy

I leave for lunch at 11:30. That way I beat the noon crowd, which is important because I only take a half-hour and am always jumpy and in a hurry to get where I'm going, eat, and get back. Where I'm going is usually the food court under the Pioneer Square shopping complex. One day it's Chinese, the next day it's Mexican, the third day it's a ham sandwich—then I start over. Occasionally there are cookies. Cookie days are the ones I most look forward to.

Jitters

It seems I've gotten a case of the jitters—mostly the stomach kind. I'm nervous and tense—not about anything in particular, but about everything in general. I noticed the other morning when I was walking to my car that my teeth were clenched and my shoulders were hunched up under my ears. It was like I was frozen in the middle of some sort of electrocution.

Jokers

Where have all the practical jokers gone—people like Gary Lohman, Jay Easton, and Glen Doyle. I never particularly cared for them, but they were, if nothing else, a sign of life. They were like those canaries in the coal mines—as long as they were there and making noise, you knew there was oxygen to breathe. But something started happening to them about four or five years ago—they began to disappear. Slowly, surreptitiously, they were weeded out by the workload and the spreadsheet sadists who managed it.

Job Application

I have mixed feelings about the ones I have filled out in my life. I have never lied on them about anything. I'm not especially proud of that—although I know there is an easy case to make for myself. To me it suggests a certain timidity, a confining reverence for the truth that is really nothing but camouflage.

Jury

One of the preliminary questions—after name, place of residence, occupation, did I know anyone in law-enforcement, had I ever been the victim of a crime, had I ever been part of a courtroom proceeding before, had I ever served on a jury before—was what did I do in my spare time. I said that since I did not rob banks or molest underaged girls in it, I could not see how my answer to the question could be of any possible relevance and that I would prefer not to answer it unless, of course, in not answering it I was exposing myself to a contempt-of-court citation. Apparently in not answering I *was* exposing myself to a contempt-of-court citation so I demurred and did the best I could, saying that I did not have any "spare" time—none of us did—but in the hours to which I assumed they alluded, I would generally be found striving to be the truest version of myself that I could. We moved on to the next juror.

Jamboree

If David May's meeting was a mess, Drew Miller's was just dull and disappointing. It was his department's fault. Miller is a big man who looks like the sort of person who should be where he is. He can seem a little stiff, a little manufactured, but he has an authoritative meeting-conductor's voice that makes up for it. If he is running the show we are satisfied. If for some reason it isn't Miller at the controls, it is usually Bruce Ware. Bruce doesn't have the voice and he is about half Miller's size, but he is smart like that pimply kid you hated in math class. Between them they do a reasonably good job with these things—we pay attention, and we invariably have something to talk about on the way back to our desks. But yesterday Miller's department brought in Jeff Rogers from marketing again to give us one of his special presentations. Rogers is an entertainer. He is articulate, energetic, likeable, and funny. His presentation was, as always, flamboyant. Anyone trying to do anything after it was bound to look tired. It typically takes about a week after one of these jamborees for things to get back to normal—a week before we can content ourselves once again with the something less that we call our usual.

Jiffy

Everyone in Brian O'Donnell's camp wants to compare him to John Penney. Penney is a mythic figure in the company—a legend. He left after only three years, but he had beautiful hair, great teeth, perfect manners, and an accent. Everyone remembers him as the person most directly responsible for the times here when we felt best about ourselves. O'Donnell wants to bring those times back. He says he's a new-blood, big-picture person like Penney, not an old-guard incrementalist like Cooper. He wants to change things. He won't say how he wants to change them or what exactly he wants to change them to—just that he wants to change them and change them in a jiffy. I think he underestimates the scope of our general indifference to such blandishments.

Just-Right

The subject tonight, in addition to the lobster mousse and the kids' respective soccer exploits, was Amy Snyder's younger sister Lisa who had turned thirty-five last weekend and was still not married. Amy thought it was time Lisa started looking for a different sort of guy, a compromise version of her impossible-to-find Mr. Just-Right—especially if she was intending to have children. You could tell by the convoluted structure of certain sentences and the careful deployment of euphemisms that this was not an argument Amy was comfortable making.

Junk

Kiessling is convinced Nancy gives him only the most odious assignments—tiresome junk reports, number-crunching stuff that she knows will drive him crazy. With the sort of in-depth analysis we have all come to expect from him, Kiessling surmises that she does this because she is sexually frustrated. Today he has been complaining about a new project. Apparently it has a deadline that is impossible to meet.

K

Kafka

I remember reading a small red paperback copy of *The Trial*, liking it very much, and thinking what a luxury it was to feel persecuted. It was so much better than feeling simply ignored.

Knees

Karen thinks she is too young to be having the trouble she is having with hers, but she isn't—not really. It's all that dancing and tennis. Simple hinges—you don't think about them at all until you do, and then you think about them all the time.

Kingdom

Russell settled in quickly to his little kingdom by the sea. He was surprised by the freedom his neighbors felt to offer him advice about fixing up the place. His children came down occasionally to borrow money for one thing or another. It was always a tricky issue for him—how much did one reasonably give and how often did they reasonably give it.

Kudos

My second break is at 2:00. I spend it in the same place I spend my first break and in the same company for the same reasons. Who wouldn't love loveable old Uncle Toby? Who wouldn't offer him kudos for actions above and beyond the call of duty?

Knowing

Laura Selby always has some new information about the goings-on around here. I have no idea where she gets it all or what she plans to do with it in the end. Probably nothing. Knowing seems to be its own reward.

Kick-Start

The people supporting Brian O'Donnell say they support him because they think he will inspire us—that he will kick-start our imaginations. I don't think inspiration is really what most of us are looking for. We don't want a bigger, brighter, better, shinier something—we just want something less bad, less tedious, less depressing to think about.

Kite

I was watching a man flying one at the beach the other day. It was some sort of advanced aerodynamic design—a garish red, white, and blue bat-shaped thing that flipped, looped, and dove. It started me thinking about my own history as a flyer. I was never obsessed with kites, but I wasn't indifferent to them either. I can't remember when I lost interest in them—I would guess it was some time before the age of ten. Up until that time I had played with maybe four or five.

When I watch this grown man with his elaborate contraption, I cannot see the fun in it—not the fun required to make the sort of investment he has made. I would enjoy holding on to the end of one of those things of his for maybe five minutes, but once I'd done that, it would be years before I was interested in doing it again. I have always thought of myself as immature (mostly because of my general inability to delay gratification), but watching this man with his kite and knowing if I were tethered to it I would be bored silly caused me to think that maybe I haven't been giving myself enough credit. Maybe in some ways I am more mature than I think.

Knots

Karen and cords do not mix. If she has one on anything, it's a mess—a hopeless tangle of kinks and coils. The cords on her phone at work, the cords for her various battery chargers, the cord on her hairdryer—they all are twisted and curled into tight, impossibly snarled knots. I can't really figure out how she actually does it. I could understand a twist here or an entwined length there—that's to be expected—but these elabo- rate, wiry fits defy comprehension.

Kindness

It's a quality I admire greatly. I am surprised when I

find myself surprised by its rarity as it's a rarity for me to think of myself as this romantic and naive.

Kowtow

Amy will not concede it is possible that Lisa may not want to have her own versions of precious little Frick and Frack—even though she has made several not-so-subtle suggestions that this might be the case. She is annoyed at Lisa for putting her in the position where she must be the voice of reason, the one who advocates such a cold, calculating, unglamorous thing as compromise, the one who kowtows to expedience. She does not want to think of herself this way, but concern for her sister's happiness has left her no choice.

Kaput

Tracy wants to believe John Kiessling is like this because his girlfriend left him, because a long-term relationship is kaput and he is sad and lost. Who is going to tell her that he is like this because he is like this? There is no missing girlfriend, no weeping when he hears a favorite song, no calendar full of significant dates. If she wants to feel sorry for him, she should probably come at it a different way—something crushing from his childhood perhaps.

Keep Thinking

I keep hoping to find a simple description of a problem that seems to me hopelessly complex, but I haven't yet. I keep thinking maybe it's just me, that I am not smart enough in some particular way or not trying hard enough, but I suppose I should consider the possibility that this sort of salubrious description simply does not exist.

L

Lights

She leaves them on and it drives me crazy. There is the waste, which disturbs me on several levels. And there is the fact that when one burns out I will have to borrow Doug's ladder because our ceilings are so fashionably high that I can't get to them with my sad little stepstool. Doug is one of those easygoing people with large wrists. He will be happy to loan me the ladder, but before he does he will have to tell me about the last time he used it.

Losing It

Funny, as much as I dislike this job and am sure continuing in it is unhealthy, I find the idea of losing it simply paralyzing. I can't imagine gathering the energy or the enthusiasm to look for another one.

Liked

I don't think Russell ever really liked his son-in-law. He never said anything explicitly disparaging about him, but he never said anything even remotely flattering either.

Local

The first thing I do when I get home is sit down in front of the television and watch a half-hour of local news. There is always a story about an automobile accident, a shooting, and some person or group being offended by something the mayor has decided to do. Then we get to the important part—the weather forecast. Tomorrow it's going to rain.

Likenesses

The list is long. We prefer showers to baths (who doesn't), dogs to cats, liberals to conservatives, wine to beer, English majors to business majors, football to baseball, long hair to short, breakfast to lunch, each other's company to the company of others.

Loans

Karen and I are city people at heart. We lived downtown for almost fifteen years. We were lured away by low-interest loans, but not too far away. We're only about a twenty-minute drive from the old apartment. We like it here—we like it here a lot—but we are still city people at heart. We would move back in a minute if we could afford to, but we can't—not now—not with all of our new requirements.

Look

Samantha Ingerson—Amy Snyder's fourth best friend—is one of those women who is always trying out a new look. We have probably met four or five times, but I never recognize her. Every time we are re-introduced it makes me think for a moment that I have started to lose my mind.

List

Dennis Parker wants Michael Tower to put him on his list of Ten Best Young Prospects. It's true that Dennis is isolated and out of touch, but he is not so isolated and out of touch as to be unaware of how much the higher-ups like lists these days. If Dennis is on the list, he is automatically somebody (as opposed to nobody); and if he's somebody, he can get a better interim project; and if he can get a better interim project, he can get a better exploratory team project; and if he can get a better exploratory team project, maybe he can move from the department he is in to the one he thinks he should be in where he could devote himself wholeheartedly to the pursuit of entre-preneurial excellence.

Letters

Adell Watson is one of those mothers who want her children to get involved with the world. She has them writing letters to various celebrities about medical care for the poor, school funding—whatever. She is a menace to society. She encourages these toxic little tots of hers to confuse talk with action and sancti-mony with humanitarianism.

Logo

The company has begun a study of its logo. Professionals

are involved. Decisions have to be made, but nobody wants to make the final one so the options proliferate and the enthusiasm for the project fades.

Lawsuits

I suspect we are involved in a number of them, but I don't really know for sure as the company is very good about keeping that sort of thing quiet. Occasionally I will get a request from some obscure department for some inconsequential document whose only possible relevance to anything we're involved with would have to be jurisprudential—but that's about it.

Loyalty

It is not loyalty to the company but credit-card debt that keeps most of us here lashed to our lovely retro-fitted workstations.

Lucky

I always think something is going to go wrong. If it doesn't, I feel I have simply been lucky.

Lotion

Karen is always smearing herself with it—hands, feet, face, legs. Apparently once you start doing this you can't stop—if you do, something terrible happens.

Lukewarm

Gary Meinhart's lukewarm support for Helen Cooper goes like this: if Cooper gets the job there is a chance—albeit a small one—that certain important things could get done. If O'Donnell gets the job, there is no chance they could get done at all.

Losses

Amy wants to know how long Lisa can continue to go from one disastrous relationship to another before she realizes she might have to do something about examining her expectations and limiting her losses. Lisa thinks she will be happier with Mr. Just-Right than with Mr. Right-Enough, but she is running out of time to be happy in. Amy's argument is that someone is ultimately better than no one.

Leftover

It is my hope that no matter how far we go we will never reach the point at which we can imagine answering all the questions we can ask because it is in that little leftover space, that sinecure of ignorance, that we will preserve and nurture the last of our sustaining illusions.

Lapses

Kiessling was called into Nancy's office again. The door was closed. We have all seen it before. We know how it will go this time from the way it went last time. Nancy will begin with some general complaints about John's work product, about errors and carelessness. She will express her disappointment. She will ask John if he knows why she called him in. He won't because it could be for any one of so many things. She will run down a list of his latest lapses and end up focusing on some report he has just done for Finney or Yarberry or Davis. She will ask him to explain himself, but he won't be able to. She will demand that improvements be made, her voice getting louder and louder, but ultimately there will not be any consequences. John will be back at his desk in twenty minutes. This is something we have seen happen over and over again, and expect to see happen over and over again—that is, until Carlton finally realizes John isn't some adorable younger version of his earlier rebellious self who has just been mishandled and misunderstood, but a fully-formed incompetent who is damaging the reputation of his department and increasing the general unhappiness. That realization is at least a year away.

M

Mother

She is a gaunt woman with strange ideas about nutrition. She is obsessed with vegetables—broccoli in particular. Apparently if you eat enough of it you will live forever and have beautiful skin.

Mute

I am pretty much mute on the subject of Lisa, but Karen can't resist this sort of thing. She will have none of the lackluster arguments in favor of pragmatism, but she tries to have none of them in a nice way because she does not really believe (nor do I, for that matter) that deep down Amy means what she has been saying. Some things, Karen says, should not be subjected to a costs/benefits analysis, at least not by certain people—and those certain people, she says, include Amy and Lisa.

Mope

One thing about Russell, he never seems to mope or to feel sorry for himself. I realized that the other day when I was talking to him about our property-tax assessments. It makes me think how often I do mope and feel sorry for myself. For instance, it seems patently unfair to me that in a neighborhood where you almost never see anyone, I have to see Boyd almost every time I turn around.

Monday

The Monday Morning Meeting—it is one of our most sacred rituals. Where you sit at the table is important to the up-and-comers. On one end is the director and on the other is the men's room. Proximity is all.

Museum

Went over to the Portland Art Museum to see the new Van Gogh. It's an early piece—a muddy, earth-toned picture of an ox pulling a cart. It was donated by a local timber tycoon. Apparently there is another version. This one has a black ox; the other has a red one. It's in Amsterdam. Remove the signature and what does one make of it? More of historical than aesthetic interest.

Mustache

I found two gray hairs in mine this morning. So begins the transformation from bandito to coot.

Money

Karen has some in at least one pocket of virtually every thing she owns. Most of the time it isn't much, but occasionally—in a coat or two—there is enough for the weekend.

Metaphors

We are at their mercy. We used to be clocks; now we are computers. I think the evolution from one to the other is supposed to have been flattering.

Movies

Something inside of me has changed somewhere along the way. Last night at the movies I found myself almost crying when in the end—after overcoming an incredible number of impossible obstacles—the boy and girl were triumphantly reunited.

Maintenance

I am a car-care fanatic because I cannot stand it when something goes wrong. I am bothered way out of all proportion by any and every sort of malfunction. I pay only the most cursory attention to the manufacturer's suggested maintenance schedule because I have a schedule of my own that is considerably more rigorous. I invariably do more than is typically required, and I do it earlier. I do the big Plan B service when they call for the little Plan A, and the huge Plan C (which includes replacing the air filter, spark plugs, and transmission fluid) when it calls for B. I replace my 40,000-mile tires at 20,000 miles and my windshield wipers on every occasion. Although I am always annoyed when the time comes for something to be done—the logistics of getting a car to and from the dealership are a nightmare—I press on because I am devastated when something breaks down, when the carefully calibrated plans I have made for my life are radically altered or destroyed by a piece of machinery. It damages hours for me—sometimes days.

Memories

I approach them more with care than with reverence—in part because I have never had much faith in the sense that they help me make of the past. I might enjoy them, but I don't think you could say I truly trust them.

Made

Everyone thought the decision about who would replace Thomas Brier would have been made by now. Apparently we can expect to be sifting the scuttlebutt for some time yet.

Missing

What is it about cats—they seem always to be missing.

Marvel

Karen can and will start a conversation with anyone. She is good at it. Curious, empathetic—I marvel at the things she says to people; they seem so perfect, the sort of things I would like to have said had I been as naturally congenial, the sort of things I would have liked said to me if I had had the time and inclination to cordially respond. But me—well, I tend not to speak unless spoken to. Conversations can be started with me, but they usually don't last long or amount to very much.

Moods

I have very little control over mine. They pile on top of me like so many mattresses.

N

Nickname

His is Chuckles. It's ironic. A disgruntled, pot-bellied loner with an interest in guns, I expect him to come in here one day and start shooting people. I've been tempted to express my concerns formally, in writing, so that when it happens there will be a paper trail for my family's lawyers to follow.

Neat

I've decided to consider myself neat. I haven't in the past, but the more I see of other people's lives—their houses, their cars, their offices—the more it seems obvious that on the neat/not-neat continuum I'm considerably closer to the orderly end.

Narrow-Minded

Russell met a woman named Deborah who seemed to think he was charming, if not particularly funny. She used to work for the City. She came from somewhere high up in the Bureau of Financial Services. She was perfect—except for being narrow-minded. It was difficult for Russell to ignore this. Maybe if she had been a little more attractive it would have been easier—it usually is for men. But she wasn't more attractive.

Nightclub

I've been to a bunch and I've enjoyed myself in them, but they were never really my idea of a truly good time. The things people did, the things they sacrificed to be part of the seething late-night crowd, I did and sacrificed not to be.

Numbers

Bruce Richardson, who I know for a fact reads serious and interesting things, was telling me a story about a ridiculously young prodigy who had an affinity not only for languages but for mathematics. He said this young man had expressed, in passing, a personal preference for numbers that were almost some other number—like 99 or 199. I said I was just the opposite—those numbers that were almost some other number made me nervous; that while I didn't care for numbers that were too blatantly or emphatically themselves—100 or 200—I did, as a rule, like those that were discreetly themselves plus a little something else: 110 or 242, for example.

Neither

Anne Loranger is one of Karen's closest friends, a sort of diminutive doppelganger. They teach at the same school. They were having lunch the other day when it started to rain. Neither one of them (or their hairdos) were prepared for the downpour so when the time came to leave the restaurant, they had to improvise. They borrowed paper bags from the waitress, poked eyeholes in them, and pulled them down over their heads. Running back toward campus, they found themselves forced into a branch of the Federal Agencies Credit Union by a series of particularly brutal gusts. Before they could pull the bags off their heads a teller hit the silent alarm.

Native

Robert Couch is unflatteringly proud of being a native Oregonian. He feels in being a native that he is by definition an improvement on the non-native, and he has a strong first-come-first-serve sense of entitlement. He feels especially hostile toward the Californians who have flooded into the state over the past decade—people with Porsches, personal trainers, and macrobiotic diets who can't pronounce the word Multnomah or Willamette and find flannel shirts funny. He blames them for ruining the housing market, the voter initiative process, and the drive into town on Highway 26. He blames them for the way he feels when he can't recognize anyone at his bank or his regular pizza place.

No Nonsense

Diane Parker is one of O'Donnell's strongest supporters. A midi in Sickler's department (mid-level, mid-career), she is quasi-euphemistically described by friends as "strong-willed" and "blunt." She appeals to a small contingent here of no-nonsensers who like it told the way it is. She has been saying things about Helen Cooper that Brian O'Donnell can't—not without looking bad—things about Helen's inclination to equivocate in pursuit of consensus and obfuscate in answer to admonition. It is too early to tell if this appeal to candor is helping.

Never

Charles wants to know if I have ever listened to a band called X (I can never remember their names). I haven't, but I doubt I would like them because in the entire history of recommendations from him I have never yet liked one. What I do like, though, is listening to Charles talk about them. He always does it beautifully. Listening to X, if you listen to him, is like listening to yourself—it is to connect in some primal way, to understand every impulse, every instrumental and lyrical choice; it is to hear described with a deadly accuracy what is a small and significant place in you. He makes me wish I did like whoever it was just so I could thank him for bringing them to my attention. Tonight, though, I just want to thank him for getting us off of the subject of Lisa.

Neighbors

How did I ever get to know so many of them?

Named

Richard Capps was just named "Employee of the Month." No one knows for sure how these selections are made, but we all have our theories—none of them commending. Richard, in accordance with his nature, is taking this patronizing "honor" very seriously. He likes having his name engraved on a plaque. He feels genuinely rewarded. We have heard him on more than one occasion refer to himself as Mr. February.

Nothing

If I think about it, I can be amazed at what we, as a species, have made out of nothing. I would like to feel comforted by it as well, but I am not.

O

Office

Mine is small and gray and one-and-a-half floors away from my supervising department. I've got two phones, a computer, a fax machine, a printer, an adding machine, a photocopier, two file cabinets, a stapler, a scraggly dieffenbachia, and a clock.

Obvious

I know what an amateur I am as a photographer when I see one of my pictures. No one would ever have wondered about the thought processes involved in my selection—they will seem obvious. I'd have to be a lot better than I am and doing this a lot longer than I have been to make someone wonder about my finding possibilities in something so improbable.

Outline

Deborah had one of those sad, sordid stories of mismatched marriage, physical and mental abuse, divorce—but she didn't seem eager to tell it (a point in her favor)—and Russell, not eager to hear it, did as little probing as possible so picked up only the most rudimentary outlines of the tale.

Opinion

How much respect should I have for someone else's opinion of what I'm worth? How much *do* I have? I guess I'd have to say that the answer to both of those questions depends almost entirely on who that someone else is.

Ordinary

Richard Ransom, in the office cattycorner from me, went to Seattle last week to watch a Seahawks game. It was his friend Tim's idea. Richard was going through a rough patch, and Tim thought it might be a good idea for them to try hanging out together. They had never really done much of that in the past—much palling around. They saw each other occasionally for lunch, exchanged a few phone calls, a few emails—that was about it. A road trip—even a short one—was out of the ordinary, and it was Tim's theory that "out of the ordinary" was just what Richard needed. It seems to have done him some good, but the good it did him doesn't seem like the sort that is going to last.

Overdress

Dwight Cooley believes if he continues to overdress for the job he is in, he will be promoted. He could be right. I'm sure that's how Kevin Pratt got where he is.

Odds

I'm one of those people who do a rough calculation of the odds and conclude anything much less than 50/50 is the same thing as impossible. This is, I think, the mathematical definition of a pessimist.

Over

So many things seem over or almost over—the polar icecaps, the literary novel, favorable exchange rates, well-behaved children, the Patriot's quest for a perfect season. Over, over, over, over. What is left is fear and sadness.

Old Man

Brian Veronski's special-credit report on *The Old Man and the Sea* was pretty much what you would expect. The story synopsis seemed to be mostly his own, but the literary analysis was little more than a cobbled conglomeration of heavily paraphrased Internet enlightenments.

Personally I never really cared much for the book—I found it simple, sentimental, and self-pitying.

Karen gave her young aspirant a B+—primarily for the effort. She knew he wanted an A—in part for the grade average, but mostly for what it would suggest about her assessment of him—but she just couldn't do it. A quaint, teacherly commitment to a minimal set of standards forbade her.

Opportunity

David Nichols likes to try out his theories of this or that on you before he takes them upstairs to impress whomever. They are never anything special—just reworked statements of the obvious—but he refuses to be alerted to this. No one really tries to help him fine-tune much as he is notoriously parsimonious when it comes to passing out credit or providing proper attribution. If someone has something worthwhile to add to something he has said, they will wait and offer it to the grandees themselves when the opportunity presents.

Opened

After college Charles moved to Los Angeles where he spent ten years trying to make his living as an actor. He had some minor successes—he landed television roles as a vampire, an amnesiacal husband, the aging son of an over-protective mother, and a priest—but nothing substantial enough to sustain the illusion that he was doing something worth doing. He took the money he made from a beer commercial, moved back here, opened his audio/video store, and was introduced to Amy by one of his customers.

Overlook

I think O'Donnell would be inclined to overlook things, let bygones be bygones, whereas Helen would, in a professional way, seek to avenge certain previous wrongs. I know who Helen is and will be, but I have no idea about O'Donnell. I have no idea what his mistakes might look like, no idea what he will do when he gets pushed into that unpleasant little place where he has to prove how tough he is.

Own

They schedule us for these meetings at the last minute. They don't really care if we have something else calendared—something difficult, something important. This takes priority. It's a not-so-subtle way of letting us know who owns our day.

Otter

The animal I would be if I had to be some animal other than the one I am.

P

Party

It's Daniel's 40th birthday party. I don't really know him, but Karen does. She likes him. (She likes everyone.) She has worked with him in the past and been on a committee with him and feels sort of obligated to be here. She didn't want to go by herself so she asked me and I had to say yes because we made a bargain long ago about evenings like these, and she was holding me to it.

Positive Attitude

I wish I had one, but I don't. I've tried to have one, of course, and I've succeeded for an hour here or an hour there, but then I've answered the phone or the door or I've read the newspaper. I don't think you can really be paying attention to anything and maintain one—not without some help from a psychopharmacological imbalance.

Prophetic

The best pictures are not just of something the way it is, but of something the way it will be—there is something prophetic about them. The subject's future is visible in the captured instant.

Posed

When it comes to taking pictures of people, I can never decide which sort I like best—those that are posed or those that aren't. If you know you are having your picture taken, you will be saying one thing; if you don't know, you will be saying something else. The question, of course, is which is true. Maybe they are both true, but I suspect one is truer than the other and, in the majority of cases, that will be the unposed one. That said, the pictures I love most of Karen are all posed. My favorite was taken by a department store elf many years ago. Karen is four or five (the distinction between posed and unposed thus mediated by her age). She is sitting on Santa's lap. Bundled up in a warm coat, her big smile simply overwhelms you. It is a picture of pure joy and innocence—the joy and innocence that are at the very center of this lovely woman.

My second favorite was snapped by Karen's younger brother, Alex. He was taking photography classes at the time. Smiling again and in a red sweater, it is a wonderful picture. It's not of Karen's character as the Santa picture is, but of her characteristics. It is a warm and faithful image of her simple beauty.

Problems

Russell has conflicting feelings about Deborah. He said it was one of the problems of old age—ambiguity.

When you are young you don't know enough to feel ambiguous about much of anything, but in old age you can end up arguing with yourself about which cereal to have for breakfast. He was, he thought, forcing himself to be interested in her, and he was afraid it showed.

Prissy

I've heard about the memo from several people now. My favorite comment was TD's. She thought she found herself mentioned in it as Julia X, a person I characterized in passing as "prissy." TD says she has no problem with this characterization, that I could have said something worse, but she doesn't see herself that way—prissy. Then she asked me to sign an expense voucher. She handed me a pen and almost immediately took it back. She said she changed her mind; she wanted me to sign in black, not in blue. Prissy? Couldn't have been her.

Pets

I don't like anything you have to keep in a cage.

Pleasure

One of Karen's greatest, most consistent pleasures is simply to think of something she has never thought of before.

Pressured

There are things I'll say, but only if I'm pressured

to. I have no interest in being the voice of doom or in raining on anyone's parade, but my views about these things are what they are—which is doom-ridden and rainy—so if I am pressured I'll say what I think, which, of course, isn't anything anyone in their right mind would really want to hear. The only people who want to hear these sorts of things said are those who for some reason think it will somehow make things better if they know they are not the only ones who feel this or that way. Usually they are careful not to ask what I think about the idea because in their hearts they already know.

Promoted

The announcement said one thing—that Scott Kohler had been promoted—but everyone thinks it was something else, although we are not sure what. We think it was something else because the person Scott replaced was considerably younger and not nearly as well educated—and where Scott had an office before, he now has a cubicle.

Published

Paul Hartman thinks he understands the motivation behind "Assorted Issues" because he is an indefatigable writer of "letters to the editor." Every now and then he gets one published. He brings it in and passes it around. We admire it for about two minutes then hand it back. That seems to be enough for him. His most recent triumph involved a complaint about the local paper's inclination to side with the forces of evil—in this case, the people at the Fish and Wildlife Department who were proposing to kill a group of predatory sea lions out near Bonneville Dam.

Plans

Karen can talk to the people at the Neighborhood Homeowners Association for hours about their policies and plans. Most of the discussions lately have been about landscaping and fees, but there has also been a lot of talk about finding a new property manager—someone sharp, someone as unlike the previous property manager as possible, someone who will do something about the trees near Mill Creek.

Pill

There is always a production involved when Karen has to take one. Several gulps of water are required as well as some head tossing, some neck-stretching, and some bobbing up and down.

Physics

I don't really understand it, but I am mesmerized by the metaphors. This mesmerization goes back to my earliest days in college when, as a sentimental humanist, I was looking for arguments against determinism and I thought I found an imposing one in Heisenberg. I learned enough to spar with my liberal-arts professors and to impress the new boyfriend of my semi-ex-girlfriend, but not enough to pass myself off as a serious amateur to anyone who actually knew anything about the subject.

Poker

Karen is terrible at it. She has no poker face, and she can't shuffle worth a damn—I mean she might as well be trying to do it with her feet. She can't bluff at all. Me, on the other hand—I can bluff, but I don't. This is something everyone eventually figures out, which means I never end up winning nearly as much as I should.

Persuasion

I cross my legs, and two seconds later Gary Davis crosses his. I touch my chin, and shortly thereafter Gary touches his. He has been to another management seminar—you can smell it on him. He has been told he can improve his skills as a persuader if he can synchronize his behavior to that of his target—that if he mimics another person's gestures or speech patterns they will subconsciously find themselves favorably disposed toward him. The problem, of course, is that when it comes to this sort of thing Gary is hopelessly uncoordinated. He can never get the rhythm right. It is immediately obvious what he is doing—and immediately annoying.

Pistachio

Karen was a chain smoker when I met her, but she stopped. It was her idea. She knew it was the smart thing to do. Every morning the first thing when she woke up—one of the primest times for a cigarette— she would toss down a jigger of lemon juice. For the rest of the day—to keep her hands and mouth busy—she would shell and eat pistachio nuts. It took her three months to gain control and three more to gain perspective.

Pathetic

Cory Nelson is new to the company. Some people are comfortable being new; Cory is not. Because his discomfort reminds me of my own in similar situations, I find him particularly pathetic. I try not to, but I don't try very hard. He is looking for someone to emulate. It's nice to know it won't be me. I hope it isn't Harris. One of him is actually more than enough. It will probably take him a month to figure out who he should be having lunch with regularly.

Proportion

How much of what he says does O'Donnell believe— and if it is anything less than all of it, what does that suggest? What is the deviation to be conceded by we reasonables, the ratio to be rationalized, the proportional tipping point where one thing becomes another and a ruined hope begins its limp toward the finish line.

Perspective

Charles and I share an inclination to ignore things. I'm not sure we do it for the same reasons, but we might. What is different, though, is that Charles expects these things he ignores to eventually just go away; I do not—a point that deserves careful consideration when assessing our individual perspectives.

Picnics

They are usually more trouble than they are worth, but they can be wonderful on those rare occasions when they are not.

Perfume

Most of it should be outlawed.

Q

Quality

This is Karen's theory of clothes: quality rather than quantity. I agree, which is why I guess I sort of have a look. I don't own much, but what I do have tends to be good and go together. With minor variations, my "ensembles" get repeated frequently. There's my duffel coat with my cords, my bomber jacket with my khakis, my parka with my jeans.

Quiescence

The lack of compassion, the righteousness—these qualities seem to get in the way of everything for Russell. The weekend he spent with Deborah in Bandon was a disaster. There was her love of trinket shopping, her complaints about breakfast (she had to wait too long), and her disparagement of a favorite painter at the Second Street Gallery ("I think my grandson could do that"). Quiescence no longer seemed an option.

Quarantine

In "Assorted Issues" I suggested we should consider quarantining people who insist that you be as interested in their hobbies as they are—people like Alan Zitka in accounting. Alan is obsessed with ant colonies.

Question

The question is not what do I want to know about myself, but what do I know about myself that I wish I didn't. That I can answer this—at least partially—is something I see counting in my favor. I try not to let it go to my head.

Quiet

Apparently I am a quiet sort of person. I seem to sneak up on everyone. And when I speak, I am often asked to repeat what I just said.

Quarrel

Our old apartment building was in the news last week. A seventy-four-year-old man named Hannif Rachadi was murdered there. (He lived on the seventh floor; we had lived on the ninth.) Apparently Mr. Rachadi brought a prostitute home with him from somewhere; they quarreled, and, in the course of the evening, she killed him. She hit him over the head once with a liquor bottle, then several more times with a heavy cooking pan.

Qualms

Charles told us a story about a Mr. and Mrs. Fenton— about trying to sell them a new home-entertainment system. They showed up in his store a week ago with a list of things they wanted—a list put together from magazine clippings, things they were certain would help them transform their evenings from what they were into what they wanted them to be. Charles had most of the gear that was on their list, but, as it turned out, most of the gear that was on their list was out of their price range no matter how creatively they were able to redefine it. Charles offered to show them another system, something that was in their price range—then another, then another. They didn't like any of them. They were certain the perfect system was out there, that it existed, but that for some perverse reason Charles had been deliberately choosing not to show it to them. They took his suggestions under advisement. He hoped they wouldn't come back, but he knew they would. When they did come back he knew they would insist on covering the same ground they covered earlier—and once they had re-covered it, they would decide not on the best that they could afford (as humbly catalogued by C), but on the most popular and widely advertised. Charles had no qualms about selling it to them, but it wouldn't be something that brightened his day.

R

Reading

As a rule, I don't much like to be read to myself. This hasn't stopped me from going to things called "Readings," however (though I'm more likely to try something called "Arts and Lectures Series" or "An Evening with So and So"). Whatever it's called, if I am there, I am hoping the reading part will be minimal or nonexistent. What I want is to hear the writer talk extemporaneously about whatever it is he or she wants to talk about and to answer questions. But, of course, questions can be a problem. They are almost never any good. If you have been to entertainments like this before you know what I'm talking about. Too many get asked by people trying to sound "literary" who just bore the bejesus out of you with some long-winded thing about the aesthetics of the unreliable narrator. I like the ones that get the writer off on some barely-related tangent. Tangents are the sunshine of evenings like these.

Raspberry Trifle

Its origins are English. And here's the surprise: it's delicious. There are, the Snyders tell us, all sorts of things that call themselves trifles. Most are pretty horrible. (Much the same thing can apparently be said about the Italian dessert tiramisu.) This trifle is distinctly up-market. It's made of only the highest quality ingredients.

Range

It wasn't just the unsuccessful relationship with Deborah that started Russell thinking about moving back to the city, it was the limited range of interests he discovered among his neighbors. Apparently the talk was all housing prices and death. I wonder—can it really be an improvement to be surrounded by people like me and Boyd?

Reverence

What would the Andrew of fifteen think of the Andrew of forty-four? I don't know. Pretty much what anyone of fifteen thinks of someone forty-four, I imagine—something unflattering that is both uninformed and uninteresting. I know the Andrew of fifteen, but he doesn't know me—not even remotely. It is annoying to find his opinion treated with reverence by people who should know better.

Retirement

I find these little retirement do-das an ordeal—the cake and speeches are about equally as good, and you invariably end up having to hug people you don't even really want to be talking to.

Rings

I wear only one.

Recollecting

At what point in life should I expect to become one of those people who starts recollecting in detail to anyone who will listen—one of those people who goes on and on about the charms of that evening when their grandmother gave them a bowl of ice cream and sat them down in front of the television to watch *The Wizard of Oz* or about that time they accidentally stabbed themselves in the thigh with a Davy Crockett pocket knife.

Reconcile

It's not important to me as a practical matter to have an imaginative conception of myself—a story, if you will, about the sort of person I think I am. I reconcile myself as much as I can with the knowledge that, if nothing else, I at least have the conscience to be appalled by my behavior—and I let it go at that.

Rearrange

Randall Stewart rearranges the furniture in his cubicle every couple of weeks. He turns his desk around or moves one of his chairs over near the printer or pushes his filing cabinet up next to the rubber plant. He thinks this will help him feel like he is having a new experience here rather than the same old experience over and over again. The longer he can continue to fool himself this way, the longer he can endure.

Rumors

We don't really have that many floating around for a company this size. Every now and then one will surface (usually about some interdepartmental power shuffle), make the rounds, and prove in the end to be substantially true. When one pops up that isn't true it causes a lot of trouble because, given our history here, we are habitually predisposed to believe it. Occasionally one of the higher-ups will try to trace one of these untrue rumors back to its source, but they have never succeeded. My theory is that they have no source, that they are spontaneously generated, that they are the inevitable consequence of confining too many pyrophoric personalities in a tight, unventilated space.

Remember

Karen can't remember his name, but she thinks it started with a "D."

Removed

To the best of my knowledge no one has ever actually died on the premises, but several have had medical emergencies and been removed from the building on stretchers. Several more have had mental or legal emergencies and been removed from the building by security.

Report

Sometimes it just seems to take forever to get nowhere. This one is going in the can.

Raise

I've never asked for a raise, in part because I have always thought it was something one was given and because I have never felt underpaid—only underemployed. I have never offered the company anything more than we originally bargained for, and, as a consequence, I have never wanted or expected anything more in return.

Ravaged

The decision on Briers's old job was announced today—they are giving it to Cooper. It is interesting to see who is excited, who is depressed, and who is somewhere in between? The Cooper supporters seem happy, but not ecstatic. They had fewer illusions about what a change in management means. They would have been disappointed, but not devastated, if it had not been her. The O'Donnell supporters expected more so they feel they have lost more with this decision—their faces are longer than the faces of Cooper's crowd would have been, their moods are blacker, their forecasts more ravaged.

Resist

We have a suggestion box here, but I have never put

anything into it. I'm not sure if it is or is not the sort of thing you would expect me to resist.

Recital

I recently saw some ancient film footage of an excited eleven-year-old Karen practicing in the driveway of her Kansas City home for yet another dance recital. Dressed in a peach-colored tutu, she hops and glides through an elaborately mimed rendition of Winter Wonderland.

S

Sister

Technically I have two, but practically it's more like one and an eighth. The second was born when I was fourteen, and I have not seen her since I left home for college. She survives in my life mostly as a name—someone to whom I must send a Christmas card.

Sleep

I never get enough of it. I can't make myself go to bed before midnight without feeling cheated. Usually it's closer to one—which means six-thirty in the morning always gets here too soon.

Subject

I have taken some pretty good pictures, but I don't think you could ever say any of them were so good as to not be almost wholly dependent on their subject.

Statutory

As always I got lost trying to find my way out of the Snyders' neighborhood. It took me three tries to find my way back to Highway 217. I tried not to be too obvious—no questionable u-turns, for example—because I had no doubt were I to be pulled over by the police, a breathalyzer test would indicate a blood-Chianti level that was clearly beyond the statutory limit.

Style

I wish I was good enough to take a picture that looked like a picture taken by me. Style is limited in photography—it usually has to be paired with a motif to have any chance of being considered individual.

Sanction

I could never get Russell to be very committal about Boyd—to sanction my bias. I'd insinuate things about my feelings trying to draw him out, but he never drew. The Pendletons, however, were another story. They were Russell's neighbors on the other side. Michelle was a divorced mother of three, but it seemed like more. She ran some sort of computer business and tended not to do a very good job when she put her garbage out on Sundays. Russell found them charming.

Strike

People are talking about "Assorted Issues." It seems several have identified themselves or characters they see as themselves and are taking offense. It hasn't gotten out of hand exactly, but it is starting to look like it could so I thought I would try a preemptive strike—present Grieg with an explanation, a *mea culpa*, an apology before he called me in and wanted something more.

Slow Down

I know if I slow down something will catch me; and if I get caught, I will suffer; and if I suffer, I will give up.

Suit

I suppose I look okay in a suit, but I don't look right— the sartorial distance from my choice of casual dress is too great. I always feel a little fraudulent, costumed.

Seems

I think Grieg used to be another sort of person, but over time—compelled by the forces that compel him to be the sort of person he appears—he has become the sort of person he seems. He has ceased to be that other sort of person—if not completely, then to a significant degree. He has ceased to be him enough to make me question my assessment of who he ever was.

Suspicion

There seems no end to the number of things one has to believe are real in order to continue on, and no end to the discomfort caused by a suspicion of such believing.

Smell

Karen always thinks she smells something burning. One of these days she is going to be right, but it will be too late because I will have ignored her.

Spell

I'm going through a little spell right now. I'm nervous, tense, sick to my stomach—and this morning my hands were shaking. I've come close to feeling like this lots of times before, but I have always been able to get it under control. This is different. I can't seem to get it under control—I'll think I have, but suddenly I haven't. It has never lasted this long. And the shaking—well, it's new and it worries me.

Square Feet

It is an anomaly that my space is so large. It was a two-person cubicle, but now that Rebecca is gone it is just me. As of this morning anyway, they do not seem to have found a need to reclaim these unused square feet. But I know somewhere in the building in the middle of one of our middle manager's minds, an idea has begun to percolate.

Stockpile

Karen is a stockpiler. She finds just the right thing, then she buys several of them. We always need to have an extra and then an extra extra so we won't run out. Apparently if we run out, our life as we know it will come to a halt. We will have to get some more of whatever it is we ran out of or we will have to spend an untold amount of time and money trying to find a suitable substitute (highly unlikely) for what is now no longer available. Our pantry looks like the inside of a small convenience store. The shelves along each wall are filled with products: we have three gallons of a special tile cleaner, four bundles of paper plates, five bottles of tub cleaner, six boxes of garbage bags. We never have fewer than 24 bottles of that Italian orange drink we like. If we have fewer than 24 bottles, we have to get some more.

Snow

We had a little today. It was obviously something new to the kids visiting across the street. They "played" in it as best they could. They scooped up handfuls from flat spots and fence posts to build a foot-high snowman. They took turns posing for pictures with him.

Strategy

When the answers are being readily dismissed, fall back on the sanctity of the question.

Swim

I'm a born swimmer. I love the water. I love the feel of it, the way your everyday reality is immediately transformed the moment you slip into it. I love the exertion of swimming and the way all of you feels used-up afterwards. I started when I was very young and continued off and on until a few years ago when the opportunity to swim sort of ceased to readily present itself. I could start again, but I am reluctant because, like so many things, swimming has become something I would rather do by myself. If my chances to go swimming in general have been reduced, my chances to go swimming alone have all but disappeared.

Something

Something happened in 1919 that had an effect on me. I don't know what it was or what the effect was, but I know that because it happened I am the person I am today and not someone else. Of course I can say the same thing about something that happened in 1819, but there's no need. You get the point.

Sunglasses

I would wear them all the time if it didn't require continual explanation or feel so cravenly affected.

Souvenirs

I have several of them. There is a pencil pot made of marble that I bought in Florence. I found it in a little shop sitting along the Arno just a stone's throw from the venerable Ponte Vecchio. A pair of black stockings purchased in Paris. And then there is the ashtray Karen and I stole from Claridges in London.

Sweat

I do not like to sweat. If I am sweating I am not having a good time. If I am having a good time and I start to sweat, that time has been seriously compromised and no longer qualifies unreservedly as good.

Scale

There was a time when I used to listen to a lot of classical music, but I don't listen to it anymore. My problem is with scale, with the swelling size of the emotions this music typically seeks to produce. They are, it seems (especially among the orchestral offerings), overly large, theatrical things—either the sort of flamboyant transports one associates with a 17th century idea of religious ecstasy or the melodramatic ardors one ascribes to a 19th century idea of romantic passion—opulent, tempestuous responses that are hard to square with a contemporary sense of our place in the grand scheme of things.

T

Tired

I am tired all the time. I'm tired when I go to bed. I'm tired when I get up. I'm tired in the middle of the day. Something is wearing me out. I think I know what it is.

Testament

One of the things that is interesting to me about Russell is that he seems to be one of those rare people who has—at this time in his life anyway—no illusions about himself. It's a testament to his character and a lesson to we less fortunate ones.

To-do

I was surprised to discover I was wasting my time confessing to Grieg. He was completely indifferent to the issue of "Assorted Issues." The to-do surrounding the memo—what little there is of it—was about people and personalities, not fourth-quarter profits or year-over-year projections. He didn't have any interest in hurt feelings—in part because the man he reported to had no interest in them, but mostly I think because such an interest did not strike him as either business-like or masculine.

Tennis

I played in college. Karen did too. In fact, that's how we met—on the court. She was good for a girl—graceful, intense—but she wasn't very fast, and she didn't like being run from sideline to sideline. We came to an arrangement. Now I'm too old, slow, and injured to play at even the most minimally acceptable level. First it was a torn muscle in my forearm that I could never get right, then it was a cracked ankle. It's a beautiful game. I miss it.

Taste

Funny, I assume most people have a certain amount of taste—not necessarily a lot, but at least a bit—and when they don't, I am surprised. Several of our friends have almost no taste at all. After all this time that fact continues to fascinate me. How could they choose those chairs, that car, that coat, that vase, that movie? How could they choose one another?

Things

Every so often I will look around the house and wonder what will happen to my things when I die. I don't think about it long—it's too sad and overwhelming. Some things Karen would want, of course, and there are some nice pieces I can imagine going somewhere—but other things, useless things that have meant something to me, my coffee cup, for instance—like me, they won't be going anywhere. I have on occasion thought about mentioning this morbid inventorying to Russell, but I haven't. If it isn't something he already finds himself doing from time to time, I don't want to get him started. And if it is something he is doing, my knowing it won't help.

Theatre

I love plays, but only if they are smart—if they aren't smart I would rather they were gutted and made into movies. Unfortunately our theatre here is not really very good. It's rare that they try anything difficult, and if they do, it's rarely with the best actors. Mostly it's safe stuff—the sort of thing you can sell season subscriptions to. I would guess I've seen maybe a dozen plays here, and I've really enjoyed only two—a production of Pirandello's *Six Characters In Search of an Author* and a Tom Stoppard play titled *Arcadia*. With each lousy experience it seems I become less interested in the form, less likely to return. It has been almost three years since my last visit—that was to see a play called *Proof*. It was proof to me of something— probably that my play-going days are numbered.

TSA Employee

It's remarkable, the pettiness of this new breed of totalitarian who thinks it is more important that their procedures should be followed than that our hair should be shiny and conditioned or our skin made safe from the sun.

Tangent

Karen is always off on one. I don't think she has ever in her life gone straight from Point A to Point B in a conversation. The sheer number and nature of the tangents and digressions can be boggling. There are digressions within digressions, and digressions within digressions within digressions—and more. Sometimes it feels like you need to leave a trail of breadcrumbs to find your way back to the beginning of things. It's not unusual for her to get lost herself.

Time

I always know what time it is even when I have no need to—or maybe I should say, especially when I have no need to.

Transition

We are waiting for one. We have been under the influence of an arctic air mass. Temperatures are supposed to moderate near the end of the week, but first a front containing a certain amount of moisture will be passing through. Exactly when it passes through and how much moisture it will ultimately contain will determine what the transition looks like—that is, how much snow and ice we will have—and what the transition looks like (*i.e.,* how much snow and ice we will have) will determine for an as-yet-undetermined amount of time what our lives will look like with regard to our normal daily routines.

Tone

Sometimes I have one—it just sort of sneaks in. I can't

say exactly what it is, but I can say that it isn't one that suggests I would be happy to listen to more of whatever it is I had just heard.

Throne

I just bought a new chair. My old one was starting to look pretty ratty—the arms were splitting, the springs were sagging. It was messing up the otherwise lovely ambiance of the living room. This new chair—a sinfully soft, cordovan-colored, leather throne—is bigger than the old one and more luxurious. The old chair—which wasn't particularly expensive—lasted almost twenty years; this new one—which is expensive and incredibly well made—could last twice that long. There is a chance it could be my last chair—the chair I will die in.

Trumpet

I have noticed that most of our buskers are busts. They tend to be musicians who cannot play. (One especially annoying example can be found torturing a trumpet every afternoon over on the corner of 4th and Salmon.) I keep running into one guy, though, who is actually quite remarkable. He doesn't have a regular spot—he moves around. He spray-paints himself silver, mounts a small pedestal, and between a series of frozen sculptural poses, juggles crystal balls.

Tantalize

On the way home Karen and I entertained ourselves by analyzing the Snyders' marriage yet again. Was

it possible, we wondered, given Amy's implied definition, that Charles had ever been her Mr. Right or
was it more likely that he had been simply Mr. Right-
Enough. The answer that tantalized seemed as obvious
as it was discomfiting.

Tonsils

I still have mine.

U

User

It's entirely possible that there are too few intravenous drug users in my life—at least that's the feeling I get from Stephen who has a life full of them. According to him, if you are not personally acquainted with someone who's in prison for murder, then you are not leading a vital, authentic life. If your girlfriend hasn't burned you with a cigarette or stabbed you in the buttocks with a penknife, then you are not living at the white-hot center of it as you should. But then, of course, Stephen is a romantic.

Uneventfully

One day I see the "For Sale" sign, and fifty-seven days later (the current average time on the market) it is gone—and so too, uneventfully, is Boyd.

Uplifted

Russell is planning a trip to France. He has always wanted to go. He knows I have been there and would live in Paris if I could, so he brings the subject up regularly as he works out his itinerary. He wants to know what he should see. To be uplifted, I tell him the Louvre, of course (ignore the Mona Lisa, spend time in the Rubens room); to be amazed by a fantasy, Mont-Saint-Michelle; to be emotionally overwhelmed, the American cemetery in Normandy.

Underway

Helen announced her choice for second-in-command this morning—big-nosed Bill. No surprise there. What was a surprise, though, were some of her comments about a plan for a certain investment program, a program with which she has been closely identified as she had tried several years ago to broker an ambitious overhaul of it and had gotten nowhere. The new plan she alluded to sounded a lot like her old plan, but with some bits and bobs tossed in from the O'Donnell camp. She was, I think, telling everyone that things were changing, that she wasn't the same old Helen but a new and improved one—one who could take other points of view into consideration, one who had a willingness to listen. This was part of a larger, more general effort underway to allay the fears of disheartened O'Donnell supporters—fears that with Helen's ascendancy we were destined for a well-worn rut. No one wants them to despair—it's bad for the bottom line.

Umbrella

Frank Hamel is one of those Oregonians who is very proud of not owning an umbrella. There are a number of them around. It's a backdoor boast about hardiness

I guess, but I don't see that there is really anything special to admire about a willingness to get soaked. It doesn't seem to have made any of them better people. It certainly hasn't made any of them more interesting.

Unanswerable

For me, the best way psychologically to confront an essential but unanswerable question is to avoid it. This does not, however, seem to be the most frequently recommended way as it suggests a certain lack of manly engagement.

Upset

Karen's appetite is connected to something central in her. She never loses it—not even when she is sick or upset.

Unpleasant

Jason Davis, an obsessive comber of old reports, likes to think of himself as an idea man—he's always coming up with something. Usually the something he keeps coming up with isn't very good—that is, it doesn't or won't work. Often it's just something that makes things unpleasant for people who already have things unpleasant enough.

Unabridged

You have to be careful what you ask Richard in technical services. He has a weakness for the unabridged reply.

Understand

Charles is not classic Mr. Right material—he doesn't have the profile, the physique, or the brooding temperament for it. He is, however, a good man—something Amy is obviously proud of having instinctively understood from the beginning—a good man who is smart, who makes her laugh, and who loves her. A rare man in that he doesn't seem to feel he has anything to prove.

Ubiquity

Gary Blake, Grieg's understudy, is everywhere—a ubiquitous presence, he roams the department regularly setting everyone's nerves on edge. He is the flag management likes to show. They think it's good for productivity.

Uniform

I would find it very difficult to wear any sort of uniform. My general feeling is that one's clothes should say as little about them as possible—but as it is impossible for them to not say anything, what they do say should be true. A uniform is in most cases a lie, and, as a consequence, it is a miserable thing to contemplate being stuck in.

Urgent

I am no good with urgent things. A tense and impatient person already tyrannized by time, I am always disturbed and a little bit destroyed by anything that must be done immediately.

V

Vendetta

I don't know what his name is, but he is taller than I like people to be and married to a woman who is much younger than he is. He parks his spectacularly ugly blue car in front of our house and leaves it there where I have to look at it every day. I have left notes on his windshield asking him to please move the thing occasionally so I could look at something else once in a while, something less forlorn, but he has not responded. A week ago I emptied a jar of honey on his hood.

Vestige

I had my picture taken today for the company newsletter. I was part of the team that put together a flamboyantly involved but useless new report. I felt like a fool sitting there with a copy of the report propped up in my lap. Who is that soulless drone, and what is he trying to smile about? Is there a vestige of the essential me in that shot? I hope not.

Variables

I hate it when the choice is not clear, when the variables proliferate, when things can turn out well or poorly depending on I don't know what.

View

If Russell has no illusions about himself, neither does he have any about the future, which he expects to be filled with an incredible assortment of natural and man-made catastrophes. He keeps this view pretty much to himself as he doesn't want to drive his friends, acquaintances, and family away with his grim prognostications, but occasionally something will slip out in conversation—an allusion to drug-resistant bacteria or global warming, for example.

Vegetarian

I have always wanted to be one in principle, but never in fact. I like the idea of it, but I'm put off by the air of piety that surrounds so many practitioners. And then, of course, there is the trouble you have to go to and the deprivation.

Vending Machine

Judging from the vending-machine offerings, you would think this company was populated by potato-chip addicts. There seem to be a dozen varieties offered—regular name-brand stuff and lesser, more esoteric things like White Cheddar Multigrain or Maui Onion. In contrast, the cookie selection is pathetic.

There are a couple of standard items from substandard producers, but nothing you could really call known. I have, at some expense, worked my way through the cookie selection and have settled on some chunks of toffee-flavored balsa wood as the best thing provided with which to periodically reward myself.

Vigilant

My day as I am obliged to arrange it is a marvel of psychological engineering—an intricate and impossibly complex system constructed to keep me functioning at some sort of minimally acceptable level. I am ever vigilant. Mostly I am looking for the little things that might go wrong—the lost set of keys, the broken coffee cup, the complaining phone call, the line I might get stuck waiting in for lunch. I am looking for the little things that go wrong because I have found it is not so often the big thing going wrong (although it can be) that leads to the occasional catastrophic collapse of the project as it is the unforeseeable interaction of trivialities.

The unfortunate thing is that no matter how vigilant I am I will never be vigilant enough. I will never be able to prevent these periodic failures. They are inherent in this sort of enterprise. Of course the fact that I can't prevent them from happening does not mean that I will not try to prevent them from happening—I will. I will also try to ignore as best I can the fact that this trying doesn't really make any sense.

When the system does fail—as it must—and I have one of those little episodes of mine, I know I'll find a way to move on, a way to get over it. I know I'll find a way to get over the next one as well, and the one after that. What worries me is the toll this sort of thing takes on one's resilience. It doesn't seem like something one should expect to be able to do forever.

Verbatim

Karen can never repeat anything she has heard verbatim. She can't even get close. As for being able to tell a joke—forget about it. What she does to a punchline is criminal.

Viable

One of the additional good things about having a really good good friend is that he or she can take the place of three or four average friends and thereby reduce the general number of friends required to be considered viable by the psychiatric crowd.

Variance

Amy didn't grow up expecting the same thing other girls did—at least not entirely. The variance—while not wholly defining—was nonetheless significant. Her focus on the world in front of her was diffused by academic interests. When they first met, Charles was just a nice guy who liked listening to her.

Vow

The Newcombs moved in this weekend. There are four of them: he and she along with little him and her. I have vowed to ignore the hideous possibilities they present.

W

Wine

I had a glass after work with egg-shaped John. It was a pinot noir from California. It was good, but nothing exceptional—still, John wanted to talk about it. He wanted to discuss its plumminess, its relation to the great vintages, its structure, its concentrated black-fruit flavors, its glycerin levels. He is one of those people who is not smart but who is desperate to seem smart, so he specializes. Besides wine, he knows way too much about Gustav Mahler.

Wrong

Apparently the Newcombs have names of which they are very proud. They shout them from the front porch day and night. RANDALL. JULIA. JUSTIN. BRITTANY. What can you say about this thoughtless breach of the peace—it's just wrong.

World

Think of the energy you would have if you were certain about the world. You could and would do things—things other than worry, that is.

Wind

The weather forecasters are trying to get us excited. There are two windstorms on the way—one after the other—and they want us to be afraid, prepared, and watching their coverage for the latest updates. They are reminding us of everything. We should have water ready and flashlights. We should avoid downed power-lines. We should be sure our children are not crushed in their sleep by falling trees.

Warning

Myrna, one of Grieg's many assistants, has started talking to herself. She's a busy person who has been getting busier, and talking her way through fax trans-missions, account entries, and supply requisitions helps her focus. This habit can be very disconcerting, however, because the transition she makes between conversations—between those she has with herself and those she has with someone else—is usually abrupt and without warning. You never know when to start or to stop listening to her.

Worry

I think I know what I'm worried about, but I have to admit there is a chance I don't. I could be wor-ried about something else—so, of course, I'm worried about that.

Wife

Almost no guy I know deserves the wife he has. There

are a few cases, of course, where the reverse is true, and fewer still where neither obtains—but, as a rule, we owe and we know it.

Whistle

I've never been able to whistle worth a damn. There was a time when I wanted very much to be able to. I wasn't interested in doing tunes—it was those shrill, piercing summons and alerts that you had to put two fingers in your mouth to make happen that attracted me. Practice though I did, it was not to be.

Want

It's nice from time to time to entertain the fantasy that somehow miraculously you no longer want what you want. That through some conscious act or spectacular piece of luck, you have been liberated from being who you are. That somehow in managing to balance the conflicting consequences of a more virtuous set of itches, you can avoid the bleak choices offered between frustration and exhaustion.

Wears Out

You should see Karen and me in a canoe. Two captains—we just spin in circles until one or the other of us wears out.

Why

A car just pulled up somewhere out front. Why do I want to see who it is? If I see who it is, it will just bother me. I can't help myself. I go upstairs and look out the window. Why are they parking there? Why not farther down the street? Why not closer to where they belong?

Washed Up

It seems Tony Matsuda didn't particularly care for "Assorted Issues." He said it was repetitive and not nearly as funny as the memo I wrote last year titled "Hot Topics." He says I'm all washed up as the office satirist. He might be right—just because I can't remember him ever having been before doesn't mean he couldn't be this time.

Wesley

My life would have been very different if I had been named Wesley.

Wiring

Karen worries about the wiring in the house. She always thinks something is going to go wrong with it while we are at work and that a fire will start in the walls. We will come home to a smoldering pile of two-by-fours and memories. A reporter from Channel 8 News will be standing out front with a microphone wanting to ask us how we feel.

Wondering

I've been wondering a bit lately about how often I seem to find myself thinking the wrong things. I wonder about Russell—did he ever go through a spell like this? Was it something he worked through, something he got over in time?

Walls

The walls of David Paling's office are bare, the bookshelves empty. If it weren't for a few papers stacked neatly on his desk, you would have no idea the space was occupied. The center of the department's universe, it is a cold, sterile place, a place that tells you in no uncertain terms that the man in charge—a disembodied presence—cares for nothing and no one. It's a place that tells you you are on your own.

Wonderful

Is there anything more unambiguously wonderful than a swing? There is for Karen. She gets motion-sick.

Wait

Without question a four-letter word. I just can't do it—not graciously. It's not so much a matter of my being unable to delay gratification (although that is certainly a part of it), it's the sense of wasting time, the most precious of all nonrenewable resources,that tortures me—of doing nothing when I could be doing something, something that in some way might at least have had the possibility of mattering.

Wistful

Karen and I spent the conclusion of our late-night ride

home from the Snyders reminiscing—gazing wistfully out into the middle distance at the history of our own marriage; marveling and shaking our heads as always at the unwarranted blessings of fortuity.

X

Xenophobia

I'm afraid of what strangers will want from me so I avoid them as much as I can. I have been avoiding them more lately than I used to, and I hope to avoid them even more in the future—if Karen will let me.

Xylophone

You would think given the general scheme of things here that one of the Newcombs might play the xylophone. This is not the case. Musically, they seem a talentless crew.

Xmas

The Murphys down the street have a tradition of getting together with their family on Christmas and watching videos they have taken of themselves getting together on other Christmases. Dinner, tree, opening presents—dinner, tree, opening presents—dinner, tree, opening presents: the wardrobes and hairstyles change, but little else. When John told me about this I said it all sounded very postmodern. He just gave me that look.

X-Ray

Photography at its creepiest.

Y

Years

I like the even-numbered ones. It has something to do with a deep-seated love of symmetry.

Yuck

I ran into Justin this afternoon when I was setting out the garbage cans. He showed me his infected toe. Yuck.

Yard

When did I start caring about mine? It must be one of those rites of passage—like your first day at school, getting your driver's license, getting married. It's the divide between being young and not being young. One day you don't even know your yard exists, the next day you're down at the nursery buying some-thing to poison the snails that have been eating your viburnum.

Yell

I am not a yeller. I can get loud now and then and

approach the decibel borderline when I am particularly upset, but these are rare, anomalous occurrences.

Yoga

I have never considered yoga. Inner peace, higher states of consciousness, a profound understanding of the nature of existence—these are clearly beyond me, as are most of the contorted meditative postures.

Yolk

After all these years I am still trying to make up my mind about eggs over-easy: do I like the yolks runny or not. Usually not, I'd say, but there are occasions when runny is fine, even preferable. It seems to depend on the hour, what is on the plate with the eggs, and my mood. It's something I have always felt I should have a stronger opinion about.

Yellow

Karen loves those little yellow post-it notes. She puts them on everything—not just one or two, but several. This morning she went to work with one stuck to the back of her blazer. It read "Library, Cleaning, Ice Cream."

Yoo-Hoo

"Yoo-hoo, is anybody home?" That is the indefatigable Mrs. Pettit out front calling to Karen who she can see on the porch manicuring one of our potted boxwoods. She wants to talk to her about a project

the Homeowners Association has been looking into—
the installation of remote-controlled gates at the
entrance of the development on Fern Ridge and the
exit on Justus.

Yo-Yo

I was once—back in my single digits—a yo-yoing
phenom. Regularly on Sunday afternoons, I would
amaze my not-especially-discerning grandmother with
an extensive array of tricks. Rock The Baby, Sleeper,
and Around The World were her favorites.

Yourself

Russell is a regular reader of a newspaper column
titled "The People's Pharmacy." An ardent do-it-
yourselfer when it comes to healthcare, he is always
passing on tips: beet juice will lower blood pressure;
spicy gumbo is good for migraines; tea can cause leg
cramps; coconut macaroons will cure chronic diar-
rhea; if you pee on your feet it will stop them from
smelling.

Young

I can't help thinking that if I had just been a little
older when I was young, I would have been much
better at being whatever it is I am now.

Z

Zorro

When I was six I wanted to be Zorro. I had the hat, the mask, the cape. I also had a small plastic sword tipped with a piece of chalk so I could put my mark on things. I have a picture somewhere of me in full regalia. I'm standing in our livingroom with my friend Dexter. Dexter is dressed as a sailor. He has an arrow through his head.

Zigzag

Justin and Brittany are playing some sort of game—part tag, part hide-and-seek. They run zigzagging between the bushes and trees in our front yard. Perhaps someone could kidnap them. They could be kept in a secluded storage facility somewhere—not long, just until their parents agreed to sell the house and move back to California.

Zillion

Karen likes to exaggerate—she's confessed to it at least a zillion times.

Zing

I hate to say it, but I don't really think there is a place for me in fiction. I'd make an awful character. My aversion to conflict and the respectfulness with which I indulge that aversion makes me inherently undramatizable. There is no rising action in the story of me; nothing is set in motion by an exciting force because exciting forces are invariably neutralized by my incessant, quasi-pathological cautiousness. There are no crises, no clash of opposing wills (no me against me, me against you, me against them), no zingy denouement, no satisfying explanation, no soothing final glimpse of order restored—there is only the voluminous incoming and time—time to watch my eyebrows bloom wild, time to tame my queasy stomach.

Zeal

Why do we want to be the Snyders' fourth best friends? Because we are zealots who believe fervently in the arguments that suggest we should.

Zoom

I like to use the zoom lens when I take pictures. I like the distortion, the sense the viewer gets that I have gotten close to something when I haven't.

Zell's

I took my watch into Zell Brothers this morning to have the battery replaced. I had to leave it. How do they think I am going to manage the rest of my day? I might as well have left them my brain.

Zoo

Neither Karen nor I like zoos. We think of them as retirement homes. The inmates are invariably bored to the point of stupefaction. They have nothing to do. Fed, watered, sheltered—they simply exist in their spaces from one day to the next. If only they could be taught to play bingo or shuffleboard—something, anything.

Zombie

I think I am coming down with something. I can feel it in my throat. Of course I am trying not to come down with it—I'm taking Vitamin C, sucking on herbal lozenges, putting some sort of zinc-laced goo up my nose—but I doubt I will be successful. I am one of those people who when he gets sick, gets really really sick—so this intimation that something is on the way is very disturbing. I can't help but be a little depressed as I pre-experience in imaginative time what I will be going through in real time—the transformation from one thing to another, from a relatively sentient being (with all the attendant capabilities) to some sort of dribbling, zombie-like individual unable to do anything but suffer. Once I've gotten whatever it is I'm getting, it will be forever before I can think about anything other than how bad I feel. When the inevitable hopes for a quick recovery are cruelly quashed by the realities of day five, I will descend into the slough of despond where I will try to ignore what I cannot ignore—namely, that no matter how physically or emotionally vigorous I may feel, I am never at any time more than a single stray microbe away from utter devastation.

Zero In

It would be nice, don't you think, if just once I could zero in on an answer that wasn't accompanied by another more disturbing question—if I could come up with something that eliminated or at least significantly reduced the consistent need to come up with something yet again.

Zone

I'm in one, but I haven't a clue as to how it should be defined.

K. B. Dixon's work has appeared in numerous magazines, newspapers, and journals. The recipient of an Individual Artist Fellowship Award from the Oregon Arts Commission, he is the author of *The Sum of His Syndromes*, a novel, and *My Desk and I*, a collection of short stories.